The First Sting

A TORLAN TARSEN ADVENTURE

The First Sting

Russell V McFall

Ordained Path Books

Published by **Ordained Path Books**
For permissions or inquiries, contact:
ordainedpathbooks@gmail.com

Cover illustration and interior artwork generated by AI under direction of the author.

First Edition

ISBN (Paperback): 978-1-972724-17-0
ISBN (Hardcover): 978-1-972724-19-4

Printed in the United States of America.

Version 1.00 -- April 2026

Dedication

To those who understand that every choice carries weight—
and that what is built, step by step,
will one day stand on its own.
May we all choose wisely.

Contents

Dedication vii
Chapter 1 — The Climb 1
Chapter 2 — Someone Who Understands 10
Chapter 3 — The Right People 15
Chapter 4 — Where It Shifts 21
Chapter 5 — Hearthridge 25
Chapter 6 — The First Reinforcements 29
Chapter 7 — The Structure Holds 34
Chapter 8 — The Entry Point 38
Chapter 9 — The First Response 45
Chapter 10 — The Man Who Notices 51
Chapter 11 — Testing the Signal 57
Chapter 12 — The Approach 64
Chapter 13 — First Contact 69
Chapter 14 — The Hook Sets 74
Chapter 15 — The Buyers Arrive 78
Chapter 16 — Terms of Control 83
Chapter 17 — The Draft 89
Chapter 18 — The Review 94
Chapter 19 — Execution Begins 100
Chapter 20 — Pressure Builds 105
Chapter 21 — The Ask 112
Chapter 22 — The Cost 122
Chapter 23 — The Strain 131
Chapter 24 — The Edge 140
Chapter 25 — The Lock 149
Chapter 26 — The Turn 156
Chapter 27 — The Doubt 165
Chapter 28 — The Commitment 175
Chapter 29 — The Collapse Begins 182
Chapter 30 — The Realization 190
Chapter 31 — The Reveal 199
Chapter 32 — The Consequence 208
Chapter 33 — The Fallout 216
Chapter 34 — Closing the Door 225
Epilogue — The Second Door Opens 232

What Happens Next... 239
Also by Russell McFall 240
About the Author 243
A Note to the Reader 244
A Final Thought 245

Chapter 1 — The Climb

The morning settled quietly over the Tarsen estate.

Light moved across the open ground in long, even lines, catching the edges of the gravel paths and the low fencing beyond. The buildings below the rise sat in their usual order—clean, purposeful, and still. Nothing had been added for appearance. Nothing had been left unfinished. It was a place that reflected the man who had built it.

Inside, the house held that same quiet.

Alex stood near the long table, reviewing the short list in front of her. The tablet in her hand displayed a handful of names, most already dismissed. A few remained.

One in particular had drawn her back more than once.

Elias Rowan.

She read through the entry again, slower this time.

Transport. Cargo. Atmospheric. Shuttle-class.

Her eyes moved back up the list, then down again.

"That's more than a driver," she said.

Across the room, Bill looked up from where he stood near the window.

"Then there's a reason he's here."

"That's what I'm thinking."

She set the tablet down lightly on the table but did not move away from it. Something about the name—and the way the experience had been written—didn't sit in the usual place. Not wrong. Just… out of place.

A soft chime sounded at the entry.

Alex straightened slightly. "That'll be him."

Elias Rowan stood just inside the doorway, hat in hand. He waited rather than stepping forward, as though he were accustomed to letting others set the tone of a room before entering it fully.

"Mr. Rowan?" Alex said.

"Yes, ma'am."

"I'm Alex. Come in."

He stepped forward, removing his hat.

Bill approached from the side. "Bill Arden."

Elias gave a small nod. "Sir."

They sat.

The first part of the interview moved easily.

Alex asked the questions. Elias answered them without hesitation, but without excess. He did not try to impress. He did not elaborate beyond what was asked. When he spoke about experience, it was in terms of what needed to be done, not what he had accomplished.

Alex noticed that.

Most people with that level of experience found a way to mention it.

He did not.

"And your most recent position?" Alex asked.

There was a slight pause—not long, but enough to register.

"I was with a settlement," Elias said. "Hearthridge."

"How long?"

"About eighteen years."

Alex glanced briefly at Bill.

He had not moved. Not even slightly. But she had worked with him long enough to recognize when he was paying attention to something specific.

"What changed?" she asked.

Elias looked down for a moment, then back up.

"We had a difficult stretch," he said. "Supplies were running behind. Equipment wasn't holding up the way it should."

He paused, as if deciding how much to include.

"We brought in outside help."

"Who?" Bill asked.

"A company that handles settlement recovery."

"Did it help?"

"For a while."

The answer was simple.

Too simple.

Alex let the silence sit for a moment before continuing.

"They provided funding," Elias said. "Equipment. Accounting. Security."

"And then?" she asked.

Elias's hands rested loosely together.

"There were problems," he said. "Supplies didn't always match what was listed. Some things didn't arrive. But the reports said everything was in order."

"Did you raise it?" Alex asked.

"Yes, ma'am."

"What happened?"

"They said the system accounted for it."

Alex held his gaze for a moment.

He believed that.

Or at least, he had.

Bill spoke again.

"And the contract?"

Elias nodded once.

"We followed it."

There was no emphasis in the statement. No defensiveness. It was simply the truth as he understood it.

"We met the terms," he said.

"As best we could."

The pause carried more weight than the words.

"There was a clause," Elias continued. "Performance thresholds."

"One miss?" Alex asked.

"Yes, ma'am."

She leaned back slightly.

One.

"And then?" Bill said.

"They took control."

Elias didn't rush the explanation.

"They were prepared. Documents already drawn up. Said it was temporary."

A small shake of his head.

"It wasn't."

Alex studied him more carefully now.

"You lost your position?"

"Yes, ma'am."

"Your investment?"

"Yes."

She paused.

"The settlement?"

Elias gave a small nod.

What struck her most was what was not there.

No anger.

No bitterness.

No attempt to shift blame.

Just… confusion.

"I don't understand it," he said quietly.

"We followed the agreement."

Bill watched him for a moment.

"Do you still have a copy?" he asked.

"Yes, sir."

"Good."

That was all.

The interview ended shortly after.

Alex walked Elias to the door.

"We'll be in touch," she said.

"Yes, ma'am. Thank you."

He stepped out into the morning light. The door closed softly behind him.

Alex remained where she was for a moment, then turned back.

Bill was already moving.

"I'll be out for a while," he said.

She nodded. "All right."

He paused just long enough to look toward the table—toward the tablet she had set down earlier—then continued toward the rear exit.

Alex watched him go.

He had already seen something.

He just hadn't said it yet.

She returned to the table and picked up the tablet again.

Hearthridge Colony.

She opened the file and began pulling records.

Outside, Bill walked the familiar path behind the estate. The ground rose gradually toward the tree line, where the land changed character. The cultivated order of the estate gave way to something older, less shaped by intention.

Beyond the trees stood the rock face.

It had been there when he first saw the property.

It had reminded him of home.

On Cyrion, there had been places like this—stone rising out of the land, not for any purpose, but simply because it belonged there. He had climbed them often. Not for the effort, but for the quiet.

He reached the base and began upward.

Inside, Alex continued her search.

She started with the obvious.

Settlement registry.
Ownership records.
Contract filings.

Everything appeared normal.

That, more than anything, made her slow down.

She began cross-checking.

Shipment logs against receiving records.
Accounting summaries against supply reports.

She adjusted the display, narrowing the comparison window.

There.

A discrepancy.

A shipment listed as complete.

The receiving record showed partial.

She sat still for a moment, then checked another.

Same pattern.

"Once is a mistake," she said quietly.

She opened a third.

Same.

Alex leaned back slightly.

"All right…"

She pulled up the contract Elias had mentioned. It took a moment to locate the relevant section.

Performance thresholds.

Support clauses.

Dependency structure.

She read it once.

Then again.

Slower.

"…all support services must be sourced through approved providers…"

Her eyes moved down the page.

"…as designated by the managing authority."

She stopped.

"They controlled the supply chain."

She opened another file. Then another.

Different settlements.

Same structure.

Alex's expression sharpened.

"This isn't local."

Outside, Bill reached the top of the rock. He pulled himself onto the ledge and sat.

Below, the estate lay quiet and ordered. Beyond it, the land stretched outward without urgency.

Elias's voice returned.

We followed the agreement…

Bill let the words settle.

Too many things had failed.

In the same direction.

He watched the horizon for a long moment.

Not failure.

Design.

Below, Alex opened a routing log.

Funds transferred off-world.
Repeated destination.
Same clearing structure.

She leaned forward slightly.

"Helix…"

The name was partial. Buried in a longer chain.

But it was there.

Alex sat back.

"This was built."

At the top of the rock, Bill drew a slow breath.

There was no authority here to correct this.

No court.
No recourse.

He looked out over the land.

"If it was designed…"

Inside, Alex glanced once more at the data.

Same contracts.
Same suppliers.
Same failures.

"…it can be undone."

Bill stood.

When he returned, Alex was waiting. She didn't speak at first.
She handed him the tablet.

He read it once.

That was enough.

He set it down.

"That wasn't failure," he said.

Alex shook her head slightly. "No."

A brief pause.

"This is organized."

Bill nodded once.

"What do you want to do?" she asked.

He considered for a moment.

"We understand it first."

Alex watched him.

"And then?"

A faint shift in his expression—barely there.

"Then we use it."

Chapter 2 — Someone Who Understands

Alex had already moved ahead of the first layer.

By the time Bill returned from the rock, she had identified the pattern. Not complete, but enough to see the outline of something larger.

Hearthridge was not an isolated failure.

It was one of several.

Same contract structure.

Same supply chain control.

Same collapse.

She had flagged three additional settlements with similar timelines.

When Bill stepped back into the room, she handed him the tablet without explanation. He read it once.

That was enough.

"This isn't local," she said.

"No."

"They're using the same structure in multiple places."

He nodded once.

She watched him for a moment.

"You've seen something else."

"Yes."

She waited.

"They designed the failure," he said.

Alex nodded. "That's where I landed."

A brief silence followed.

Then she said, "We're outside normal channels."

"Yes."

"No local authority. No contract leverage. No enforcement."

"No."

She folded her arms lightly.

"So what do we do?"

Bill didn't answer immediately. He looked once toward the window, then back to the tablet.

"We don't approach it directly."

Alex tilted her head slightly. "You're thinking indirect."

"Yes."

She studied him for a moment.

Then she said, "You know someone."

It wasn't a question.

Bill met her eyes. "Yes."

Marcus Venn did not look like someone who had built his life on deception.

That was the first thing Alex noticed.

He sat comfortably in the chair across from them, one arm resting along the side, the other loosely folded. His posture was relaxed, but not careless. He watched the room the way someone does when they've spent a long time understanding how rooms work.

Not suspicious.

Aware.

"You said this was about contracts," Marcus said.

"It is," Alex replied.

"And a pattern?"

"Yes."

She handed him the tablet.

He didn't rush it.

That, Alex noticed, was the second thing.

He read slowly. Not because he needed to, but because he wanted to see how it had been put together.

After a moment, he nodded once and handed it back.

"All right," he said. "That's clean."

Alex leaned forward slightly. "Clean?"

"Too clean," Marcus said. "Same structure, same failure points. That doesn't happen by accident."

"We reached the same conclusion," she said.

"I'd be surprised if you hadn't."

He glanced briefly at Bill, then back to Alex.

"So you want to stop it."

"Yes."

Marcus nodded again, as if confirming something to himself.

"That means you're not looking for proof. You already have enough of that."

Alex frowned slightly. "Then what are we looking for?"

Marcus leaned back a fraction.

"A way in."

Bill spoke quietly.

"They rely on the contract."

"Yes," Marcus said.

"They control the system."

"Yes."

"They expect compliance."

Marcus's expression shifted slightly.

"That's where they're weakest."

Alex studied him.

"Explain that."

Marcus considered for a moment, as though deciding how much to say.

Then he said, "You don't beat something like this by pushing against it. You let it keep working."

Alex frowned slightly. "That doesn't stop it."

"No," Marcus said. "But it tells you how it moves."

He leaned forward slightly.

"What you're dealing with is a long con. They build trust. They build structure. Then they take everything when it collapses."

Alex nodded slowly. "That matches what we're seeing."

Marcus held her gaze.

"So if you want to stop them, you don't break the system."

He paused.

"You use it."

Bill said quietly, "That's what I thought."

Alex looked between them.

"You're talking about setting something up."

"Yes," Marcus said.

"What kind of setup?"

He gave the smallest hint of a smile.

"The kind where the mark thinks he's winning."

Alex leaned back slightly.

"Mark," she repeated.

"The target," Marcus said simply.

"Calder Voss," Bill said.

Marcus nodded once.

"And how do we get him to move?" Alex asked.

Marcus didn't answer immediately. Instead, he asked, "What does he want?"

Alex didn't hesitate.

"Fast gain. Low risk. Control."

Marcus nodded.

"Good."

He settled back again.

"Then we give him something that looks like all three."

Alex studied him more carefully now.

"And that's enough?"

Marcus shook his head slightly.

"No."

He looked at Bill.

"You'll need a hook. Something he can't ignore."

Bill said quietly, "We have that."

Alex looked at him.

"What?"

Bill's answer was simple.

"What he missed."

Marcus's expression sharpened just slightly.

Now he was interested.

"All right," he said.

"Now we're getting somewhere."

Chapter 3 — The Right People

The table had changed.

Not in shape or position—but in purpose. What had been a place for discussion had become something more focused. The tablet was still there, but now it was only one part of the space. Notes had been added. A few names. A few roles.

Nothing extra.

Alex stood near the end of the table, reviewing what she had already confirmed.

Same contract structure.
Same supplier control.
Same failure pattern.

It wasn't a theory anymore.

Bill stood by the window, looking out over the lower field.

"You were right," Alex said.

He didn't turn. "About what?"

"This wasn't just designed," she said. "It's being repeated."

He nodded once.

"That means they expect it to work."

Marcus sat in one of the chairs, leaning back slightly, watching both of them.

"That's because it does," he said.

Alex looked at him. "Until now."

Marcus gave a small, almost approving nod.

"Until now," he agreed.

Bill turned back toward the table.

"We need people," he said.

Marcus shook his head slightly.

"No. You need the right ones."

Alex picked up the tablet again.

"We start with the front," she said.

"The face," Marcus replied.

"Yes."

She turned the screen slightly so both men could see.

"Daniel Mercer."

Marcus leaned forward just enough to read.

"Trade negotiator. Frontier routes."

"He's worked contracts like this before," Alex said. "Not these specifically—but similar structures."

Marcus nodded once.

"He'll know how to talk without sounding like he's trying to sell something."

"That's what I thought."

Bill looked at the name for a moment.

"Will he understand what we're doing?"

Marcus gave a slight shrug.

"He doesn't need to understand all of it. He just needs to believe his part is real."

Bill held his gaze a moment longer, then nodded once.

"Bring him in."

Later that afternoon, Daniel Mercer stood where Elias had stood the morning before.

He carried himself differently. Not better. Not worse. Just more aware of how he appeared.

"Bill," he said, with a nod.

“Dane,” Bill replied.

Alex noticed that. The name shortened without discussion. It fit.

Dane listened more than he spoke. That was the first thing Marcus noticed. The second was that when he did speak, it was measured.

“You’re not asking me to convince someone of something that isn’t there,” Dane said.

“No,” Bill said.

Dane glanced briefly at Alex, then back.

“You want them to believe they’ve found something.”

“Yes.”

Dane nodded once.

“That’s easier.”

Marcus gave a quiet huff of agreement.

“We’ll need contract support,” Alex said.

Bill looked at her.

“Someone who sees structure,” she added. “Not just wording.”

Marcus nodded.

“Yes. You will.”

The next day, Lillian Kade arrived.

She didn’t bring much with her. A single case. No extra materials.

She sat, opened the contract file Alex had prepared, and began reading. No introductions beyond names. No small talk.

After a few minutes, she looked up.

“This is enforceable,” she said.

Alex leaned forward slightly. “All of it?”

“Yes.”

She paused.

“Which is the problem.”

Marcus smiled faintly.

"I like her," he said.

Lillian didn't react.

"Where does it break?" Bill asked.

She looked back down at the file.

"It doesn't break," she said.

Then:

"It shifts."

Alex watched her carefully now.

"Show me."

Lillian turned the display slightly.

"Here. Support dependency clause."

Alex read it again, then again, slower.

"They control supply."

"Yes."

"They control reporting."

"Yes."

Alex sat back.

"They control failure."

Lillian gave a small nod.

"That's the intent."

Marcus leaned forward slightly.

"So where do they lose it?"

Lillian didn't answer immediately. She moved further down the contract, then stopped.

"Here."

Alex leaned in again.

"Subsurface classification."

Bill stepped closer.

"They defined what they own," Lillian said.

She paused.

"But not what it becomes."

Silence settled for a moment.

Marcus's expression sharpened.

"There it is," he said quietly.

Alex looked at Bill. He didn't say anything, but she could see it. He had already moved past the problem.

"We'll need system support," Alex said. "Data that holds under review."

Marcus nodded.

"Yes. You will."

Joren Pike arrived that evening.

He didn't stand on formality. He nodded once to each of them and moved to the table without waiting.

Alex handed him the data set.

He scanned it quickly, then again, slower.

"You want this to look real," he said.

"Yes."

He nodded once.

"It will."

Alex watched him.

"And if it's tested?"

He glanced up.

"It'll pass."

A pause.

"Until it doesn't."

Marcus gave a quiet laugh.

"That's honest."

"We don't need perfect," Bill said.

Joren nodded.

"Good. Perfect gets noticed."

By the next morning, Mara Ellin had arrived.

Elias met her outside.

They stood for a moment without speaking.

Then she said, "We didn't miss anything."

Elias didn't answer. He didn't need to.

Inside, Mara reviewed the operational logs Alex had assembled. She moved through them steadily, occasionally stopping, occasionally nodding.

"They delayed the shipments," she said.

"Yes," Alex replied.

"Just enough."

Mara looked up.

"They planned it."

Bill stepped forward slightly.

"Yes."

The room settled—not in uncertainty, but in alignment.

Marcus looked around the table.

"You've got your crew," he said.

Bill shook his head once.

"Not yet."

Marcus raised an eyebrow slightly.

"No?"

Bill looked at each of them in turn.

"One more thing," he said.

Alex watched him.

"What?"

Bill's answer was simple.

"We make it real."

Chapter 4 — Where It Shifts

The table was quiet again.

Not empty—just settled. The names were still there. The roles. The notes Alex had layered across the display. But something had changed since the day before. It was no longer a question of whether there was a pattern.

There was.

Now the question was where it gave way.

Lillian stood near the table, the contract open in front of her. She had read it more than once. Not quickly. Not slowly. Just thoroughly.

Alex watched her without interrupting. Marcus remained seated, one arm resting lightly along the chair, his attention fixed on the same page without appearing to study it directly. Bill stood back slightly, giving space.

"It doesn't break," Lillian said.

She didn't look up when she said it.

Alex nodded. "You said that yesterday."

"Yes."

A small pause.

"It shifts."

Marcus leaned forward just slightly. "That's the part I like," he said.

Lillian moved her hand down the display. "Here."

Alex stepped closer. "Subsurface classification," she read.

Bill didn't move, but his focus narrowed.

"They've defined what they own," Lillian said.

"Yes," Alex replied.

"And they've defined what they control."

"Yes."

Lillian tapped once lightly on the screen. "But not what it becomes."

The words settled into the room.

Marcus exhaled quietly. "There it is."

Alex read the section again, then again, slower.

"They separate categories," she said.

"Yes."

"But they don't account for reclassification."

"No."

Alex leaned back slightly. "If something changes category…"

Lillian finished it. "It moves outside their control."

Marcus looked toward Bill. "That's your door."

Bill stepped forward now. Not quickly—just enough to see the section for himself.

He read it once. That was enough.

"They assumed static value," he said.

Alex nodded. "They built everything around it."

Marcus gave a small, approving tilt of his head. "That's what people like this do. They lock the structure. Then they stop looking at it."

Lillian closed the file. "They didn't expect anything new," she said.

A brief silence followed. Not uncertain. Just complete.

Alex turned slightly. "So we introduce something new."

Marcus didn't answer immediately. He looked at her for a moment.

Then he said, "Not introduce. Reveal."

Alex held his gaze. "You're splitting the difference."

"I'm keeping it believable."

Bill's attention remained on the contract. "They have to think it was already there."

Marcus nodded once. "Yes."

"And missed," Bill added.

Alex looked between them. "And valuable."

Marcus leaned back again. "Now you're speaking the same language."

He rested his hand lightly on the table. "So what is it?"

Alex brought up a new display. "Something that reads as high potential. Not fully defined. Not fully understood."

Joren, who had been quiet until now, spoke without looking up. "Energy signatures would work."

Alex glanced toward him. "Explain."

Joren adjusted the display slightly. "Deep-layer readings. Irregular, but consistent enough to look real. Not complete. Just enough to suggest something worth chasing."

Marcus gave a small nod. "Good. Incomplete is better."

Alex looked back at the data. "And it needs to sit inside the reclassification window."

Lillian answered that. "It will."

Bill looked up. "Can it hold?"

Joren nodded once. "If he checks it, it holds." He paused. "If he digs deeper, it gets complicated."

Marcus smiled faintly. "Complicated is good."

Alex didn't look up. "Complicated buys time."

Bill stepped back from the table. For a moment, no one spoke.

The plan was no longer forming.

It was aligning.

Elias, who had remained near the edge of the room, shifted slightly. "This would happen there," he said.

The others looked toward him.

"At Hearthridge," he added.

Alex nodded. "It has to."

Elias gave a small, steady nod. "That's where he'd believe it."

Marcus looked toward Bill. "He's right."

Bill didn't respond immediately. He walked a few steps toward the window and looked out over the lower field. The land beyond the estate stretched outward, quiet and unchanged.

He stood there for a moment.

Then he said, "We don't build this from here."

Alex watched him. "No."

Marcus leaned back slightly. "Good."

Bill turned. "We go there."

No one questioned it.

Lillian closed her case. Joren began adjusting his notes. Marcus stood.

Alex gathered the tablet. "When?" she asked.

Bill's answer was simple.

"Now."

Chapter 5 — Hearthridge

The transport settled in without ceremony.

No marked landing zone. No signal beacons. Just a stretch of open ground that had once been cleared and used often enough to hold its shape. The dust lifted briefly as the engines powered down, then drifted back into place as if nothing had disturbed it.

From the cockpit, Elias watched the ground through the forward pane. For a moment, he didn't move. Then he said quietly, "That's close enough."

The hatch opened with a soft release. Warm air moved in—not harsh, not difficult, but carrying a stillness that hadn't been there before. It was the kind of quiet that followed activity, not preceded it.

Bill stepped down first. He paused just long enough to take in the surroundings. Structures stood where they had been built—functional, evenly spaced—but there was a difference now. Edges that should have been maintained were worn. Pathways that had once been clear had softened. Nothing was broken.

But nothing was being kept.

Alex stepped down behind him, tablet already in hand. She didn't speak immediately. Her eyes moved across the settlement, matching what she saw to what she had already studied.

"It's intact," she said.

"Yes," Elias replied.

She glanced toward him.

"That's the point," he added.

Marcus followed, slower. He took a longer look.

"Clean exit," he said.

Alex glanced at him.

"They didn't need to damage anything," he continued. "The contract did the work."

Elias stepped forward onto the ground. He didn't head toward the buildings right away. Instead, he stood still for a moment, looking across the space as if placing things back where they had been.

"That used to be the supply line," he said, nodding slightly to the left. "Came in every third day."

Alex followed his gaze. The path was still there. Faint.

"What changed?" she asked.

Elias gave a small shake of his head. "They slowed it down. At first, just a little."

Bill began walking. No direction announced—just forward. The others followed.

The central structure was still open. Inside, the air was cooler, but carried the same sense of pause. Tables remained where they had been used. A few items left behind—nothing of value, just things not worth taking.

Alex moved along the far side, scanning quietly. "Inventory logs match what we saw. Nothing officially missing."

Marcus gave a slight nod. "That's how they do it."

Elias stepped toward one of the tables. His hand rested lightly on the edge.

"This is where we tracked incoming," he said. "Everything passed through here."

Alex looked at him. "And the reports?"

"Came from the same system."

She nodded once. "Controlled input."

Marcus added, "Controlled output."

Bill didn't speak. He moved through the room, not examining anything directly, but seeing enough.

Outside, the wind shifted slightly. Not strong—just enough to move the dust along the path.

"Bill."

The voice came from behind them.

They turned.

A woman stood near the entrance. She had stopped just inside the shade, as if uncertain whether to come further.

Elias stepped forward immediately. "Mara."

She crossed the distance without hesitation. For a moment, neither of them spoke.

Then she said, "You came back."

Elias nodded once. "Yes."

Her eyes moved past him, taking in the others. "You brought help."

Bill stepped forward. "Bill Arden."

She studied him briefly—not skeptical, not welcoming—just measuring.

"Mara Ellin," she said.

Alex stepped forward slightly. "Alex."

Mara gave a small nod, then looked back to Elias.

"We didn't miss anything," she said.

Elias didn't answer. He didn't need to.

Mara turned slightly, gesturing toward the outer structures. "They kept it running long enough to take it. After that, they didn't need it."

Alex glanced at Bill. Same pattern.

"Can you show us?" Alex asked.

Mara nodded. "Yes."

They moved through the settlement together. Each step confirmed what they already knew.

Delayed routes.

Unused storage.

Equipment left in place—but not maintained.

At one point, Mara stopped near a ground access panel.

"This is where we first noticed it," she said.

Alex stepped closer. "Noticed what?"

"The delay," Mara replied. "Supplies would register here before they arrived."

Alex's expression sharpened slightly. "They logged it early."

Mara nodded. "Yes."

Marcus gave a quiet, approving look. "That's confidence. They didn't think anyone would check closely."

Elias looked down at the panel. "We trusted the system," he said.

Alex didn't respond. She was already working through it.

Bill stood a few steps back, watching.

The pieces were no longer separate. They were in place.

Mara straightened. "You're not just here to look."

Bill met her gaze. "No."

She nodded once. "Good."

A brief silence followed.

Then Alex spoke. "We're going to need a location."

Mara looked at her. "For what?"

Alex glanced at Bill, then back.

"To make something real."

Chapter 6 — The First Reinforcements

Morning came slower at Hearthridge.

Not because the sun delayed—but because nothing moved to meet it. The light spread across the settlement the same way it always had, touching the structures, the pathways, the edges of equipment left where it had last been used. But there was no response. No sound of work beginning. No small routines picking up where they had left off the day before.

Just light… and stillness.

Alex stood near the central structure, tablet in hand. She had already begun mapping what they had seen—supply routes, storage points, access panels. Now that she was here, the data carried weight it hadn't before. What had looked like numbers now had distance, timing, gaps.

"They didn't just slow it," she said.

Bill, standing a short distance away, glanced toward her. "They spaced it."

He nodded once. "That's how you control output without stopping it."

Marcus, seated on a low crate nearby, added without looking up, "Too fast, people notice. Too slow, they adjust." He shifted slightly. "You keep it just inside tolerance… they blame themselves."

Elias stood near the edge of the open space, looking toward the supply line path. "We did," he said quietly.

No one answered that.

A faint sound reached them from beyond the outer structures. Not loud—but distinct.

Alex looked up first. "Transport."

Bill turned slightly toward the sound.

The craft came in low, controlled, and unremarkable. It didn't announce itself. It didn't need to. It settled near the same open ground they had used the day before. Dust lifted, then settled again.

Marcus stood. "That'll be your front," he said.

The hatch opened. Daniel Mercer stepped down.

He paused just long enough to take in the space. Not dramatically. Just a quick read. Then he walked toward them.

"Bill," he said with a nod.

"Dane."

Alex watched the exchange. Same as before. No introduction needed beyond that.

Dane's eyes moved across the settlement once more. "Feels recent," he said.

"It is," Mara replied from behind them.

He turned slightly. She met his gaze without hesitation.

"They didn't break anything," he said.

"No," she answered. "They didn't need to."

Dane gave a small nod. "That tells me what I need to know."

Alex tilted her head slightly. "What's that?"

Dane looked back toward the central structure. "They plan to use it again."

Marcus gave a quiet hum of agreement. "Or something like it."

Bill didn't comment.

Dane shifted his attention back to Alex. "What are we building?"

Alex didn't answer immediately. She glanced toward Bill.

He gave the smallest nod.

"Something they missed," she said.

Dane considered that. Then: "Good. That's easier to sell."

Marcus smiled faintly. "Always is."

Another sound followed—sharper this time, more mechanical.

Alex looked up again. "That'll be your system," Marcus said.

The second transport came in slightly higher, adjusting twice before settling. It wasn't rough—just precise.

The hatch opened quickly. Joren Pike stepped out without hesitation.

He didn't pause to take in the surroundings. He moved straight toward the group.

"Alex," he said with a brief nod.

"Joren."

She handed him the tablet without introduction. He took it and began scanning immediately.

"What are we trying to show?" he asked.

"Energy variance," Alex said. "Deep layer. Not fully defined."

He nodded once. "Good."

Dane glanced at Marcus. "He says that a lot?"

Marcus didn't look at him. "When it's worth saying."

Joren slowed slightly, then stopped.

"This holds," he said.

Alex watched him. "Under review?"

He nodded. "If he checks it, it holds." A pause. "If he pushes it… it gets complicated."

Marcus smiled again. "That's what we want."

Joren handed the tablet back. "You'll need live data."

Alex nodded. "We expected that."

He looked past her, toward the ground beyond the structure. "Then we should start there."

Bill stepped forward slightly. "Show us."

Joren didn't speak. He simply turned and began walking toward the outer edge of the settlement. The others followed.

They reached a section of ground where the surface had been disturbed at some point, then left to settle again. Nothing marked it clearly, but it wasn't untouched.

Joren stopped. "This is where I'd anchor it," he said.

Alex stepped beside him. "Why here?"

He pointed once, lightly. "Layer density shift. Not obvious—but enough to build on."

She looked down, then back at her tablet. The data aligned.

"This works," she said.

Dane stepped closer, looking over the area. "So this becomes the story."

Marcus nodded. "Yes."

Dane glanced at Bill. "And I sell it."

Bill met his gaze. "You present it."

Dane gave a small smile. "Same thing, if it's done right."

Marcus shook his head slightly. "Not quite."

Dane didn't argue.

Elias stood a few steps back, watching. For the first time since they had arrived, something in the space felt different. Not restored. Not yet. But moving.

Mara stepped beside him. "They're building something," she said quietly.

Elias nodded. "Yes."

She looked at him. "You trust this?"

He didn't answer immediately. Then: "I trust them."

She held his gaze a moment longer, then nodded once.

Back at the center of the group, Alex looked between the data and the ground. "It needs to look incomplete," she said.

Joren nodded. "It will."

Marcus added, "Enough to draw him in."

Dane finished it. "Not enough to satisfy him."

Bill looked at each of them in turn. The pieces were beginning to move.

"Start building it," he said.

No one hesitated.

For the first time since Hearthridge had gone quiet, something was being put into place.

Chapter 7 — The Structure Holds

By midday, Hearthridge no longer felt still.

It wasn't restored—nothing close to that—but something had shifted. Movement had returned, quiet and deliberate. Equipment that had been left idle was now in use again, though not for its original purpose. There was no noise of industry, no sense of routine returning. Just intention.

Alex stood near the central table, reviewing the first pass of the data Joren had assembled. It wasn't complete. That was by design.

She adjusted the display slightly and narrowed the output range.

"It's too clean," she said.

Joren looked up from where he stood. "Where?"

She angled the tablet toward him. "The transition. It resolves too evenly."

He studied it for a moment, then nodded once. "You're right."

Dane, standing a few steps away, glanced over. "What's wrong with it?"

"It answers too many questions," Alex said.

Marcus gave a quiet nod from his seat. "That'll get it dismissed. Or worse, examined."

Joren made a quick adjustment. The pattern shifted—not broken, just less certain.

"Better," Marcus said.

Dane crossed his arms lightly. "So we're building something that doesn't quite make sense."

Alex looked at him. "It makes enough sense."

"And leaves the rest to him," Marcus added.

Dane nodded slowly. "Right. He fills in what he wants to see."

Bill stood near the edge of the structure, watching. Not the data—the people. They were settling into place, each of them working within their role without needing it defined.

"Where does he see it?" Dane asked.

"We control that," Alex said.

Marcus shook his head slightly. "No. You guide it."

Alex paused, then nodded. "Explain."

"If you hand it to him, he questions it," Marcus said. "If he finds it, he owns it."

Dane gave a small smile. "That part I understand."

"So he doesn't see us," Bill said.

"He sees what he's already looking for," Marcus replied.

Alex lowered the tablet slightly. "Then we need to know what he's looking for."

Mara, who had been standing near the far side of the structure, spoke quietly. "He's always looking for the next gain."

The group turned toward her.

"Not long-term. Not stability," she said. "Something he can take quickly."

Elias nodded. "That's right."

Marcus considered that. "Good."

"So we give him something immediate," Dane said.

"And unstable," Joren added.

Marcus smiled faintly. "Now you're getting it."

Bill stepped forward slightly. "What triggers him?"

Marcus didn't answer right away. He looked at the data again, then at the ground outside.

"Opportunity under pressure," he said.

Alex waited.

"He has to believe that if he doesn't act now, he loses it."

Dane nodded. "That's what moves him."

Alex was already working again. "We can stage the timing. Limited window. Uncertain classification."

"I can stagger the readings," Joren said.

"Make it look like it's resolving," Marcus added.

"Then disappearing," Dane said.

Alex glanced at him. "Yes."

Mara watched the exchange quietly. "You're making it something he can't wait on."

Bill nodded once. "That's the idea."

A transport sound in the distance drew their attention. The craft came in steady and controlled, landing cleanly beyond the main structures.

Lillian Kade stepped out and moved toward them without hesitation.

"Show me," she said.

Alex handed her the tablet. Lillian read it once, then again.

"This works," she said.

Dane gave a small smile. "That's encouraging."

Lillian didn't react. She moved her finger down the display. "Here."

Alex leaned in.

"Your timing window," Lillian said, "is too wide."

Marcus nodded immediately. "She's right."

"Too wide how?" Dane asked.

"He has time to verify," Lillian said.

Alex adjusted the display. "How tight?"

Lillian considered it. "Short enough that he has to move. Long enough that he thinks it's his decision."

"That's the line," Marcus said.

Joren made another adjustment. The window narrowed.

"That feels right," Dane said.

Lillian handed the tablet back. "Now it becomes a choice."

"Not quite," Bill said.

The group looked at him.

"He needs to believe there's competition," Bill added.

Marcus's expression sharpened. "Yes. He does."

"We can layer that in," Alex said.

"Another buyer," Dane suggested.

"Not visible," Marcus said. "Implied."

"Enough to be credible," Lillian added. "Not enough to confirm."

Joren adjusted the structure again. "It's there."

A brief silence followed. The system now had shape—still incomplete, but defined.

Mara stepped back slightly, looking at the group. "You're building it."

Bill met her gaze. "Yes."

She nodded once. "Then finish it."

Bill turned back to the others. "We're close."

"Not yet," Marcus said.

Bill looked at him. "What's missing?"

Marcus didn't answer immediately. He looked at the data, then at the ground, then back at the group.

Finally, he said, "The entry point."

Alex frowned slightly. "We have the data."

"Yes," Marcus said. "But how does he hear about it?"

Chapter 8 — The Entry Point

The plan was no longer about what they would build.

It was about how it would be seen.

Alex stood at the central table, reviewing the latest iteration of the data set. The structure held. The variance readings were stable enough to pass a surface check, inconsistent enough to invite a deeper look. The timing window was narrow now—tight enough to create pressure without appearing forced.

It was ready.

But it still didn't exist beyond Hearthridge.

Dane leaned against the edge of the table, arms loosely folded, watching the display without focusing on any one point.

"So," he said, "how does it reach him?"

Marcus didn't answer immediately. He remained seated, gaze steady, as if measuring the question rather than responding to it.

"That depends," he said finally, "on how he listens."

Alex glanced up. "Meaning?"

"Some men watch reports," Marcus said. "Some rely on people. Some only move when something crosses their path that looks like opportunity."

Dane gave a small nod. "Voss is the third."

Elias looked toward him. "You're sure?"

Dane didn't hesitate. "Yes."

"Why?" Alex asked.

Dane shifted slightly, then pointed toward the display.

"Because this kind of operation doesn't run on curiosity," he said. "It runs on advantage. He doesn't go looking for things. Things are brought to him—filtered, refined, made worth his time."

Marcus nodded once. "That's right."

Alex considered that.

"So we don't send it to him," she said.

"No," Marcus replied. "We place it where it will be brought to him."

Bill, standing a few steps back, spoke quietly.

"Through someone he already trusts."

Dane looked toward him.

"Or someone he thinks he does," he said.

A brief silence followed.

The direction had shifted again—not in structure, but in approach.

Alex turned back to the display and began pulling up communication channels tied to the Hearthridge contract network.

"Approved providers," she said. "Supply chain coordinators. Financial auditors. Third-party logistics."

She paused.

"They all report upward."

Marcus leaned forward slightly.

"Show me the path."

Alex adjusted the display, layering connections between entities. A web began to form—clean, efficient, and tightly controlled.

Joren stepped closer.

"That's centralized," he said.

"Yes," Alex replied.

"Which means it bottlenecks."

Marcus gave a faint smile.

"And bottlenecks are where things slip through."

Dane nodded slowly.

"Or get inserted."

Alex looked at him.

"You're thinking we introduce it into the system."

"Not directly," Dane said. "Adjacent."

Marcus glanced at him.

"Explain."

Dane straightened slightly, now fully engaged.

"You don't alter their records," he said. "You create something that their system has to account for."

Alex's expression sharpened.

"A discrepancy."

"Yes."

Marcus nodded once.

"That's a hook," he said.

Elias stepped closer to the table.

"They'll investigate it," he said.

"Not immediately," Dane replied. "First they'll try to reconcile it."

Alex was already moving.

She pulled up a new layer—shipment logs tied to the region surrounding Hearthridge.

"We can introduce a flagged variance," she said. "Something that doesn't match existing classification."

Joren leaned in.

"It'll have to sit just outside their known categories."

"Which puts it into review," Alex said.

"And review means attention," Marcus added.

Bill watched the exchange, then asked the question that mattered.

"Who sees it first?"

Alex traced the path upward.

"Mid-level oversight," she said. "Then escalated."

Dane shook his head slightly.

"That's too slow."

Marcus looked at him.

"You want to accelerate it."

"Yes."

"How?"

Dane pointed once at the display.

"You give it weight."

Alex frowned slightly.

"Define that."

"Not just data," Dane said. "Context. Something that suggests value before it's confirmed."

Marcus's expression shifted.

Now it was coming together.

"Implied gain," he said.

Dane nodded.

"Exactly."

Alex adjusted the structure again.

"A secondary note," she said. "Preliminary assessment. High potential."

Joren added, "Unverified."

Marcus smiled faintly.

"That's the part he likes."

Elias watched the screen.

"And that reaches him?"

Dane looked at him.

"It gets close enough," he said. "From there, it depends on him."

Bill spoke quietly.

"No."

The others turned toward him.

"We don't depend on him," he said. "We guide him."

Marcus nodded once.

"That's the difference."

Alex paused, then adjusted the routing again.

"We can introduce a second signal," she said.

"What kind?" Joren asked.

"External interest," she replied.

Dane's expression shifted slightly.

"Careful," he said.

Marcus agreed.

"Too visible, and it looks staged."

Alex nodded.

"Not visible," she said. "Just enough to suggest movement."

Joren worked the data.

"It's there," he said after a moment. "Barely."

Marcus leaned back.

"Good."

Mara, who had been listening quietly, stepped forward.

"You're making it look like someone else saw it first," she said.

Alex glanced at her.

"Yes."

Mara nodded slowly.

"That would matter to him."

Elias looked between them.

"He doesn't want to miss anything," he said.

Dane gave a small smile.

"No," he said. "He doesn't."

The room settled again, but this time it carried a different weight.

The structure was no longer internal.

It had a path.

Alex looked at Bill.

"It's ready," she said.

He held her gaze for a moment, then nodded once.

"Send it," he said.

Joren didn't hesitate. His hands moved across the interface, initiating the sequence.

The data shifted from local to networked, moving along the channels they had mapped, passing through the same structures that had once controlled Hearthridge.

No alarms triggered.

No flags raised.

It entered quietly.

Exactly as it needed to.

Marcus watched the display.

"That's it," he said.

Dane exhaled slowly.

"Now we wait."

Bill shook his head slightly.

"No," he said.

They looked at him.

"We watch."

Alex's eyes remained on the data stream.

Already tracking.

Already measuring.

Somewhere beyond Hearthridge, the system had received something new.

Not enough to stop it.

Not enough to understand it.

But enough—

to notice.

Chapter 9 — The First Response

The system did not react immediately.

That was expected.

Alex watched the flow of data across the display, tracking its movement through the same structured channels that had once controlled Hearthridge. It passed through without resistance, settling into the network as if it had always been there.

"Initial entry complete," she said.

Joren nodded without looking up. "No flags."

Marcus leaned back slightly. "Good. That means it doesn't stand out."

Dane stood near the far side of the structure, watching the others more than the data.

"Standing out isn't the problem," he said. "Being ignored is."

Alex didn't look away from the display.

"It won't be ignored," she said.

"Not yet," Marcus added.

Bill stood near the entrance, looking out toward the open ground. He hadn't moved since the transmission began.

"Where does it go next?" he asked.

Alex adjusted the view, narrowing the pathways.

"Regional oversight," she said. "Mid-level review."

Joren added, "They'll try to reconcile it first."

Dane gave a slight nod. "They'll assume it's an error."

Marcus looked at him. "At first."

Elias stepped closer.

"And if they can't explain it?"

Dane's answer was simple.

"They escalate."

The room grew quiet again—not uncertain, but attentive.

They weren't building anymore. They were waiting.

It didn't take long.

"There," Alex said.

The shift was subtle—just a small change in the routing pattern.

Joren leaned in.

"That's a review request," he said.

Alex nodded.

"Originating from oversight."

Marcus gave a quiet smile.

"They saw it."

Dane crossed his arms lightly.

"Now they decide what it is."

Alex expanded the feed.

A secondary layer appeared—internal notes, partially obscured but visible enough to interpret.

"Preliminary classification mismatch," she read.

Joren added, "Unresolved variance."

Marcus nodded once.

"That's curiosity."

Dane shook his head slightly.

"Not yet," he said. "That's irritation."

Alex glanced at him.

"Explain."

"They don't like things that don't fit," Dane said. "First they try to fix it. Then they start asking why it won't fix."

Marcus gave a small nod.

"And that's when it becomes interesting."

Elias watched the screen.

"They'll send someone?"

"Not yet," Alex said. "Still internal."

Bill turned slightly from the doorway.

"How long?"

Alex considered.

"Depends on how quickly they run out of explanations."

Joren adjusted the feed again.

"They're cross-checking supply logs," he said.

Mara, standing near the far side, spoke quietly.

"They won't find anything."

Alex nodded.

"No. They won't."

Another shift followed—small, but different.

Joren leaned in again.

"That's new."

Alex focused on the update.

"Secondary annotation," she said.

Marcus straightened slightly.

"Read it."

Alex scanned it once, then again.

"Potential energy variance," she said.

Dane's expression changed slightly.

"There it is."

Marcus nodded.

"Now it has value."

Bill stepped closer to the table.

"Who wrote it?"

Alex traced the source.

"Mid-level analyst," she said. "No direct authority."

Dane gave a small smile.

"Perfect."

Elias frowned slightly.

"Why?"

"Because he's guessing," Dane said. "And if he's guessing, he'll want to be right."

Marcus added, "People take risks when they think they've found something first."

Alex watched the feed.

"He flagged it upward."

Joren confirmed.

"Escalation request."

A brief silence followed.

Then Marcus said quietly, "Now we see who picks it up."

The system shifted again.

Not data this time.

Attention.

Alex adjusted the view.

"It's moving faster now," she said.

Joren nodded.

"They skipped a level."

Dane looked at Marcus.

"That's interest."

Marcus shook his head slightly.

"That's competition."

Elias looked between them.

"I thought you said that comes later."

Marcus gave a faint smile.

"It usually does."

Dane added, "Unless someone doesn't want to lose it."

Alex tracked the routing.

"It's been redirected," she said.

"To where?" Bill asked.

She paused.

Then said, "Private review channel."

Marcus leaned back.

"Well now," he said.

Dane's tone was quieter.

"That's closer."

Elias looked at the display.

"Closer to who?"

Alex didn't answer immediately. She followed the path carefully, confirming each step before speaking.

Then she said, "Closer to him."

No one needed the name.

The room held steady.

Bill's voice was calm.

"Does he see it yet?"

Alex shook her head slightly.

"Not directly."

Marcus added, "But someone who matters does."

Dane nodded.

"And that's enough."

Mara looked between them.

"This is what you wanted."

Alex didn't take her eyes off the display.

"Yes."

A moment passed. Then another.

Joren spoke quietly.

"They're tagging it."

Alex leaned in slightly.

"With what?"

Joren read it off.

"Priority review."

Marcus gave a small, satisfied nod.

"That's your hook."

Bill looked at the screen.

It had begun.

Not with force. Not with confrontation.

But with attention.

"Stay on it," he said.

Alex didn't respond. She already was.

Somewhere beyond Hearthridge, a system that had operated without question had just been given one. Not enough to stop it. Not enough to expose it.

But enough—

to make someone look twice.

Chapter 10 — The Man Who Notices

The report did not belong where it was.

That was the first thing Adrian Kessler understood.

He did not need to read it twice to know that. The classification alone told him enough. It had bypassed the normal reconciliation queue and appeared in a channel reserved for priority review. That did not happen without cause.

Or without error.

Kessler sat back slightly, eyes still on the display.

"Show me the origin," he said.

The system responded immediately, tracing the path backward through the network. Each step appeared clean—properly logged, properly routed.

That, more than anything, held his attention.

Nothing in the chain was wrong.

And yet something was.

He leaned forward again and opened the attached data.

Energy variance.

Preliminary.

Unverified.

He frowned slightly.

"Unverified doesn't come here," he said.

Across the room, a junior analyst looked up.

"It was flagged during reconciliation," she said. "Mismatch in classification."

Kessler didn't look at her.

"That would send it sideways," he said. "Not up."

She hesitated.

"It escalated," she said. "Twice."

That got his attention.

He shifted the display, isolating the annotation trail.

Mid-level analyst.

Initial flag.

Secondary note.

Potential value.

Kessler's eyes narrowed slightly.

"Who added that?" he asked.

The system highlighted the entry. A name he didn't recognize.

That didn't matter.

The behavior did.

He tapped the display once, bringing up the full dataset.

It was incomplete.

That was intentional.

He could see it in the way the variance moved—consistent enough to suggest structure, inconsistent enough to avoid definition.

Not noise.

Not random.

Constructed.

Kessler leaned back again.

"Interesting," he said quietly.

Across the room, the analyst spoke again.

"Do you want it reassigned?"

"No."

The answer came without hesitation.

He studied the data again, this time more slowly.

"Where is it?" he asked.

"Hearthridge sector," she said.

Kessler's expression didn't change, but he registered the name. He remembered it—not clearly, but enough. A settlement that had transitioned out of active status. Controlled acquisition. No irregularities reported.

Closed.

"Bring up the contract," he said.

The file appeared.

He didn't read it in full. He didn't need to.

He moved directly to the structural clauses.

Support dependency.

Performance thresholds.

Control transfer.

All standard.

All clean.

Then he stopped.

Subsurface classification.

He read that section once.

Then again, slower.

"They didn't close that," he said.

The analyst frowned slightly.

"Close what?"

Kessler didn't answer immediately.

He continued reading.

The clause defined ownership.

Defined control.

Defined limitation.

But it assumed stability.

He leaned back.

"That's a problem," he said.

"For them?" she asked.

"For whoever didn't notice it," he replied.

He turned his attention back to the variance report.

Energy signature.

Deep layer.

Unverified.

If it was real, it changed the classification.

If it changed the classification, it moved outside the existing structure.

Kessler sat still for a moment.

Not deciding.

Calculating.

"Who else has seen this?" he asked.

The system responded.

Limited access.

Restricted channel.

Two additional views.

He studied the names.

One he recognized.

The other he didn't.

"Have they acted on it?" he asked.

"No directive issued," the analyst said.

Kessler nodded once.

That meant hesitation.

Hesitation meant opportunity.

He closed the contract file and returned to the variance.

The data still bothered him.

Not because it was wrong.

Because it was almost right.

He tapped into the underlying structure and ran a quick verification pass. The system responded as expected.

No failure.

No contradiction.

But something held.

Something that resisted full resolution.

He exhaled slowly.

"They built this carefully," he said.

The analyst looked at him.

"Who did?"

Kessler didn't answer.

Not yet.

Instead, he opened a private channel. The interface shifted, access narrowing.

He hesitated for just a moment.

Then tagged the report.

Priority review.

The system acknowledged the change. Routing adjusted. Visibility expanded—slightly.

Kessler watched the update settle into place.

"If this is real," he said quietly, "it won't stay here."

"And if it isn't?" the analyst asked.

Kessler's expression didn't change.

"Then someone wanted it to be seen."

He closed the display.

"Keep it quiet," he said.

"Yes, sir."

He stood.

Not quickly.

Not with urgency.

But with intention.

As he moved toward the exit, he paused just long enough to look back at the screen.

Hearthridge.

Closed systems were supposed to stay closed.

This one hadn't.

He stepped out into the corridor.

Somewhere along the line, something had been introduced.

Not forced.

Not obvious.

Placed.

Kessler allowed himself the smallest hint of a smile.

"All right," he said under his breath.

"Let's see what you are."

Chapter 11 — Testing the Signal

Kessler didn't let it sit.

That was the difference.

Most would have waited—let the system resolve it, let someone else decide whether it mattered. That was how errors passed through unnoticed.

He didn't trust the system that way.

He trusted what resisted it.

"Pull the deeper layer," he said.

The analyst hesitated.

"That's restricted," she said.

"I know," Kessler replied.

There was a brief pause.

Then she moved.

The display shifted, opening access beyond the standard reconciliation data. The structure beneath the report came into view—rawer, less refined, not meant for quick review.

Kessler leaned forward slightly.

"Let's see what you are," he said quietly.

At Hearthridge, Alex felt it before she saw it.

A subtle shift in the data flow—nothing obvious, nothing disruptive. Just a change in the way the system moved through their construct.

She looked up.

"He's pushing," she said.

Joren was already watching.

"Deeper access," he confirmed.

Marcus, seated nearby, didn't move.

"Good," he said.

Dane frowned slightly.

"Good?"

Marcus nodded once.

"If he wasn't, we'd have a problem."

Bill stepped closer.

"What does it change?"

Alex didn't answer immediately. Her eyes moved across the display, tracking the access path.

"He's not looking at the surface anymore," she said. "He's going underneath."

Joren added, "He's testing structure."

Elias looked between them.

"Can it hold?"

Joren didn't hesitate.

"Yes."

He paused.

"Mostly."

Dane exhaled slowly.

"I don't like 'mostly.'"

Marcus glanced at him.

"You don't get perfect," he said. "You get believable."

Alex adjusted the view.

"He's isolating the variance," she said. "Trying to resolve it."

Joren nodded.

"I expected that."

"Can he?" Elias asked.

Joren shook his head.

"Not completely."

Alex added, "He'll get close."

Marcus leaned forward slightly.

"And when he does?"

Alex met his gaze.

"He'll see what we want him to see."

Back in the review channel, Kessler narrowed the scope.

The deeper data did not contradict the surface report.

That was the problem.

If it had failed cleanly, he would have dismissed it. If it had resolved cleanly, he would have passed it along.

It did neither.

He adjusted the parameters again.

"Run a layered comparison," he said.

The analyst complied.

The system processed and returned.

No direct conflict.

But no full alignment either.

Kessler sat back.

"That's deliberate," he said.

The analyst looked at him.

"You think it's fabricated?"

Kessler didn't answer immediately.

He studied the structure again.

"Not fabricated," he said finally.

"Constructed."

At Hearthridge, Alex stilled.

"He said it," she murmured.

Joren glanced at her.

"What?"

"He knows," she said.

Marcus shook his head slightly.

"No," he said. "He suspects."

Dane crossed his arms.

"That's worse."

Marcus gave a faint smile.

"No. That's exactly where we want him."

Bill looked at Alex.

"Can he prove it?"

She shook her head.

"Not with what he has."

Joren added, "He'll try to force it."

Marcus nodded.

"And when he can't?"

Alex answered.

"He'll escalate again."

Back in the channel, Kessler changed approach.

If the structure wouldn't resolve cleanly, then the answer wasn't inside it.

It was around it.

"Cross-reference external activity," he said.

The analyst hesitated again.

"That's outside the file."

"I know," Kessler said.

"Do it anyway."

At Hearthridge, the shift hit harder this time.

Alex's head came up immediately.

"He's widening," she said.

Joren leaned in.

"Looking for context."

Dane muttered quietly, "Here we go."

Marcus's tone remained calm.

"Hold it steady."

Alex moved quickly, adjusting the data pathways.

"Secondary signal is holding," she said.

Joren checked it.

"Barely."

Bill stepped closer.

"What happens if it breaks?"

Joren didn't look up.

"Then it looks wrong."

Elias frowned.

"And that ends it?"

Marcus shook his head.

"No," he said. "That exposes it."

The room tightened slightly.

Alex slowed her movements.

"Don't overcorrect," Marcus said quietly.

"I'm not," she replied.

He watched her for a moment, then nodded.

"Good."

On the other side of the system, Kessler reviewed the external layer.

There it was.

Not obvious. Not direct.

But present.

A secondary signal.

Unconfirmed. Unclaimed.

He leaned forward again.

“Someone else saw it,” he said.

The analyst looked up.

“Who?”

Kessler shook his head slightly.

“Doesn’t matter.”

It mattered to him.

Competition changed everything.

If another party had noticed the same variance, then delay carried risk.

Kessler closed the external view and returned to the core file.

“This isn’t going to resolve on its own,” he said.

“No,” the analyst agreed.

He made the decision.

“Prepare a field request,” he said.

She blinked.

“For verification?”

Kessler’s answer was calm.

“For acquisition.”

At Hearthridge, Alex froze.

Then she said, “He’s moving.”

Joren looked up.

“How far?”

Alex’s voice was steady.

“Field-level.”

Dane let out a slow breath.

“That’s fast.”

Marcus nodded once.

“That’s commitment.”

Bill looked at the display.

“Can we handle it?”

Alex didn't hesitate.

"Yes."

There was a brief pause.

Then she added, "But it just got real."

The room settled again—but not in the same way as before.

The plan had worked.

Now it had to hold.

Chapter 12 — The Approach

The decision moved faster than the data.

Alex saw it in the shift before the confirmation came through. The routing tightened, the access narrowed, and then a new layer appeared—logistics.

She leaned slightly closer to the display.

"They've initiated movement," she said.

Joren glanced up. "How far along?"

"Early stage," she replied. "But it's real."

Marcus, seated near the table, nodded once. "That's your field request. Converted."

Dane crossed his arms lightly. "Not verification. Acquisition."

Alex gave a small nod. "Yes."

Bill stood near the entrance, watching the open ground beyond the structures.

"When?" he asked.

Alex checked the timeline. "Soon. They're not waiting."

Marcus gave a faint smile. "They never do when they think they're first."

Elias looked toward the outer edge of the settlement.

"They'll come direct?" he asked.

Dane shook his head slightly. "No. Not at first."

Elias frowned. "Why not?"

"Because they don't trust what they haven't seen," Dane replied. "They'll send someone ahead. Quiet. Observing."

Marcus added, "And measuring risk."

Alex adjusted the display again. "Two-stage approach. Advance contact, then acquisition team."

Bill turned slightly. "Which means we have less time."

"Yes," Alex said.

The room shifted again. Not planning. Preparation.

Dane stepped forward, resting one hand lightly on the table.

"All right," he said. "This is where it changes."

Marcus looked at him. "Yes."

Dane glanced around the group.

"We're not just building something now," he said. "We're presenting it."

Alex met his gaze. "Walk it through."

Dane nodded once.

"They come in cautious. First contact is controlled—questions, not commitments. They're looking for inconsistencies."

Joren gave a small nod. "They won't find any."

"Good," Dane said. "But they'll assume they missed something."

Marcus added, "Which keeps them looking."

Dane continued.

"We don't push. We let them come to it."

Elias watched him. "And if they don't?"

Dane gave a slight smile. "They will."

Mara, standing near the far side, spoke quietly.

"They'll want control."

Dane nodded. "Yes."

He looked back at Alex.

"So we let them think they can take it."

Alex adjusted the display. "Controlled access. Limited exposure."

Joren added, "Staged readings."

Marcus nodded. "Just enough to confirm. Not enough to satisfy."

Bill stepped closer.

"Who meets them?"

The question settled into the room.

Dane didn't answer immediately.

Then he said, "I do."

Elias looked at him. "As what?"

Dane's tone was steady.

"Someone already involved."

Marcus gave a small nod. "That works."

Alex tilted her head slightly. "What's your angle?"

Dane thought for a moment.

"Independent contractor," he said. "Brought in late. Not fully trusted. Not fully informed."

Marcus's expression sharpened slightly. "Good. That gives you room."

Bill looked at him. "Room for what?"

Dane met his gaze.

"To be wrong."

A brief silence followed.

Marcus gave a quiet laugh. "He understands."

Alex studied Dane more carefully now.

"You'll need support," she said.

"I know," he replied.

She glanced at Joren. "Live feed."

Joren nodded. "Continuous."

She looked at Lillian. "Contract positioning."

Lillian gave a small nod. "Ready."

Marcus leaned back slightly.

"And me," he said.

Dane glanced at him. "Yes. You."

Marcus's faint smile returned.

"I'll stay where I belong."

Elias looked between them. "Where's that?"

Marcus's answer was simple.

"Just outside the picture."

Bill turned back toward the open ground.

"They'll be here soon."

Alex checked the timeline again. "Yes."

The settlement felt different now. Not empty. Not abandoned.

Occupied.

Dane moved toward the entrance, stopping just short of stepping outside. He looked across the structures, the pathways, the ground where Joren had anchored the variance.

"You built this well," he said.

Alex joined him. "It will hold."

Dane nodded once. "It needs to."

Behind them, Marcus spoke quietly.

"It will."

Dane didn't turn. "Because of the data?"

Marcus shook his head slightly. "No."

A small pause followed.

"Because of the man who's about to walk into it."

The words settled into the space.

Bill stepped forward again.

"When they arrive," he said, "we stay in control."

Dane nodded. "Yes."

Alex added, "Without appearing to."

Marcus gave a faint smile. "Now you're learning."

A soft alert sounded from the system.

Joren looked up immediately. "Contact."

The room stilled.

Alex stepped closer to the display. "Confirm."

Joren's eyes moved quickly across the data. "Advance unit. Single craft."

Elias looked toward the horizon. "Already?"

Dane's expression didn't change. "They're faster than most."

Bill's voice was calm.

"Positions."

No one rushed. They moved with purpose.

Dane stepped outside.

The wind carried lightly across the open ground as he walked toward the center of the settlement.

Behind him, the others took their places—seen or unseen, present or implied.

The structure they had built now extended beyond data.

It was real.

In the distance, a small craft broke the horizon—low, controlled, direct.

Dane stopped and waited.

For the first time since the plan had begun, someone else was stepping into it.

Chapter 13 — First Contact

The craft came in low and steady, controlled in a way that suggested experience rather than caution. Dane watched without moving. The approach told him what he needed to know—no hesitation in the descent, no deviation in the line. Whoever was flying it had done this before.

That was expected.

The craft settled just beyond the central structures with minimal disturbance. Dust rose briefly, then fell back into place. There was no announcement, no signal. The hatch opened, and one man stepped out.

Dane did not move to meet him immediately. He let the distance remain.

The man paused at the base of the ramp, taking in the surroundings. His gaze moved across the settlement—not casually, not quickly, but with purpose. He wasn't looking for what was there. He was looking for what wasn't.

Dane started forward then, closing the distance at a measured pace. Not eager. Not delayed.

They stopped a few steps apart.

"Didn't expect anyone already here," the man said. His tone was neutral, professional. Not unfriendly, but not open.

Dane gave a slight nod. "Same could be said."

The man's eyes shifted, measuring.

"You're working this site?"

"Part of it."

A brief pause followed.

"Name?"

"Mercer."

The man considered that.

"Contracted?"

"Late-stage," Dane said. "Brought in after things started shifting."

That landed.

The man nodded once. "Graham."

No last name. That was fine.

They stood in silence for a moment. Not uncomfortable. Just deliberate.

Graham glanced past Dane toward the structures. "Didn't think this place was active."

"It isn't."

Another small pause.

"Then what are you doing here?"

Dane let the question sit before answering. "Trying to understand what was missed."

Graham's expression didn't change, but his attention sharpened.

"That's not your contract."

"No," Dane agreed. "It isn't."

Graham shifted slightly. "Then why take it?"

Dane gave a faint shrug. "Because it didn't sit right."

That was enough.

Graham studied him for a moment longer. "What did you find?"

Dane didn't answer directly. Instead, he glanced briefly toward the ground beyond the structure—the area Joren had marked—then back.

"Something incomplete."

Graham followed the glance, just for a fraction of a second.

That was all Dane needed.

"Incomplete how?" Graham asked.

"Depends on how you read it."

Graham stepped forward, not toward Dane but slightly past him, angling his view toward the open ground.

"Show me."

Dane didn't move. "Not sure that helps either of us."

Graham stopped and turned back.

"Why not?"

Dane held his gaze. "Because if it's nothing, you've wasted your time. If it's something, you'll want control of it."

Graham didn't respond immediately.

That was the moment.

He understood.

"Who else knows?" Graham asked.

Dane shook his head slightly. "Not many."

"Not many isn't none."

"No. It isn't."

Graham's eyes narrowed slightly.

"Then I'd suggest you show me."

Dane considered him, just long enough, then turned.

"Walk with me."

Behind the structures, Alex watched the exchange through the live feed. No audio lag. No signal disruption. Everything clean.

"He took it," she said quietly.

Marcus nodded. "Of course he did."

Joren monitored the data stream. "His system's already recording."

Alex didn't look away. "Let it."

Outside, Dane led Graham toward the marked ground. Not directly—at a slight angle, with a slight delay.

"Settlement didn't fail the way the reports say," Dane said as they walked.

Graham didn't respond.

"Supply records don't match delivery. Equipment logs don't match usage."

"That happens," Graham said flatly.

"Not like this."

They reached the edge of the area. Dane stopped. Graham stepped beside him.

For a moment, neither spoke.

Then Dane said, "It's under there."

Graham looked down. Nothing visible.

"Based on what?"

"Readings. Deep layer."

Graham didn't move. He didn't kneel or scan. He simply stood there, thinking.

"If you're wrong," he said, "this ends here."

Dane nodded once. "I know."

"And if you're right?"

Dane met his gaze. "Then this doesn't stay here."

A long pause followed.

Graham looked back at the ground. Then, finally, he moved.

He pulled a compact scanner from his side, activated it, and ran a quick pass across the surface. The device responded—not fully, not cleanly, but enough.

Graham's eyes shifted slightly. "There's something."

Dane didn't respond.

He didn't need to.

Graham ran the scan again, slower this time. The same result.

He straightened.

"Who else has seen this?"

"Not many."

Graham nodded once. "That's about to change."

Dane held his gaze. "I figured."

Graham stepped back.

"This site is now under review."

"Understood."

Graham turned toward the craft, then paused.

"One more thing," he said without turning back.

Dane waited.

"If you're playing this wrong… you won't get a second chance."

Dane's answer was steady. "I'm not."

Graham didn't respond. He continued walking. The hatch closed. The craft lifted, then disappeared.

Dane stood alone for a moment before exhaling slowly.

Behind him, the wind moved lightly across the ground.

Inside, Alex looked up from the display.

"He's convinced."

Marcus shook his head slightly. "No. He's interested."

Dane walked back toward the structure.

"That's enough."

Bill met him at the entrance.

"How close?"

Dane's answer was simple.

"Closer than before."

Chapter 14 — The Hook Sets

The report didn't stay where Kessler left it. It moved—not through normal channels, and not slowly. The priority tag shifted its path, narrowing the number of people who could see it while increasing the weight of those who did.

Kessler noticed the change immediately.

"Who pulled it?" he asked.

The analyst checked the routing. "Executive filter."

Kessler leaned back slightly. That meant one thing. Someone above him had taken interest.

He didn't try to retrieve it. That wasn't how this worked. If someone higher had decided to look, then the report had already passed the point where control was possible. The only thing left was to understand what they saw—and what they might do next.

He opened a secondary channel and began tracking the movement indirectly.

"Keep monitoring," he said. "Anything that branches from it, I want to see."

"Yes, sir."

Across the system, the report settled into a quieter space—more restricted, more deliberate.

Director Halvern did not rush. He read the report once, then again more slowly, not because it was complex, but because it was incomplete in a way that didn't sit comfortably.

Energy variance. Unverified. Potential value.

He leaned back in his chair.

"Where did this come from?" he asked.

An assistant standing nearby responded, "Hearthridge sector."

Halvern's expression remained neutral. "Closed site."

"Yes, sir."

He looked at the data again. Closed systems did not generate new value—not without cause.

"Who flagged it?" he asked.

The assistant checked. "Mid-level analyst. Escalated through two channels. Then Kessler."

Halvern nodded once. He knew Kessler—careful, precise, not prone to overreaction. If Kessler had allowed it to move, then it had resisted explanation.

That made it worth his time.

"Pull the external context," Halvern said.

At Hearthridge, Alex saw the shift immediately.

"It's moving again," she said.

Joren leaned in. "Higher?"

"Yes."

Marcus, seated nearby, gave a small nod. "Good."

Dane glanced toward the display. "Define good."

Marcus didn't look at him. "It means we've reached someone who can act."

Bill stepped closer. "Can they see through it?"

Alex shook her head. "Not yet."

Joren added, "They're still reading."

Back in the system, Halvern reviewed the external layer. There it was—subtle, unconfirmed, but present.

"A second signal," he said.

The assistant hesitated. "Unverified."

Halvern nodded. "Of course it is."

He leaned forward slightly. "If this were clean, it wouldn't be here."

He adjusted the parameters, running a comparative scan across historical data tied to the region. No matches. No prior flags.

That increased the value.

"Who's on site?" he asked.

The assistant checked the logs. "Advance contact unit. Graham."

Halvern nodded once. Reliable. Not imaginative. That was useful.

"Status?" he asked.

"Preliminary review complete. Site flagged."

Halvern considered that.

"Flagged for what?"

The assistant hesitated. "Acquisition."

Halvern's expression didn't change. "Good."

He closed the external view and returned to the core report.

"If this is real, we move now," he said.

"And if it isn't?" the assistant asked.

Halvern looked at her. "Then we confirm that before anyone else does."

At Hearthridge, Dane stood just inside the structure, listening as Alex relayed the movement.

"They've escalated again," she said. "Higher authority."

Dane nodded slowly. "That didn't take long."

Marcus gave a faint smile. "It never does once it matters."

Elias looked between them. "So what happens now?"

"They commit," Dane said.

Alex added, "Or they pull back."

Marcus shook his head slightly. "They won't pull back."

Bill looked at him. "Why not?"

"Because they're already imagining what they gain."

A brief silence followed.

Joren spoke quietly. "They're preparing logistics."

Alex checked the feed. "Yes."

Dane exhaled slowly. "That's your acquisition team."

Mara stepped forward slightly. "How many?"

Alex narrowed the data. "Small. Efficient."

Marcus nodded. "They don't need numbers. They need control."

Bill turned toward Dane. "When they arrive, what changes?"

Dane met his gaze. "Everything."

He stepped toward the table, placing both hands lightly on its edge.

"The first man asks questions," he said. "The second man makes decisions."

Elias frowned slightly. "And which one is this?"

Dane's answer came without hesitation. "The second."

The room settled again—not uncertain, not unprepared, but focused.

Alex looked at the display one more time. "They're not waiting."

Bill nodded once. "Neither are we."

Outside, the wind shifted slightly across the open ground. The settlement no longer felt abandoned. It felt like something else entirely—a place where something was about to be decided.

Chapter 15 — The Buyers Arrive

The second craft did not come in quietly. It wasn't loud or aggressive, but it didn't hide its approach the way the first had. Its path was direct, its descent deliberate, and its presence unmistakable.

Dane saw it before the others said anything.

"They're here," he said.

Alex didn't look up from the display. "Confirmed."

Joren added, "Multiple signatures. Three onboard."

Marcus, seated near the back, gave a small nod. "That's enough."

Bill stepped toward the entrance, eyes already on the horizon.

"Positions," he said.

No one rushed. They moved with purpose, each to the place they had already chosen.

Dane stepped out first. The open ground stretched ahead of him, unchanged, quiet, waiting. He stopped near the center of the settlement and let the distance settle again, just as he had before.

The craft descended and touched down with controlled precision. The hatch opened, and three figures emerged.

The first stepped down with the ease of someone accustomed to being followed—neither hurried nor cautious, but certain. Dane didn't need an introduction. This was the one.

The second remained half a step behind, observant and measuring. The third stayed closer to the craft, scanning the perimeter without appearing to do so.

Dane started forward, again not eager and not delayed.

They met at a distance that allowed space—but not comfort.

"You're Mercer," the lead man said. His voice carried authority without effort.

Dane gave a slight nod. "I am."

The man studied him longer than Graham had, not looking for information but for weakness.

"I'm Halvern," he said.

Dane inclined his head slightly. "Director."

That registered—a small thing, but not missed.

Halvern's gaze shifted briefly past Dane, toward the structures and the ground beyond.

"Your preliminary contact was… adequate," he said.

"Graham is thorough," Dane replied.

Halvern gave a slight nod. "Yes. He is."

A brief silence followed.

Then Halvern said, "Show me."

No lead-in. No negotiation.

Dane didn't move immediately.

"Depends what you're looking for," he said.

The second man shifted slightly. Halvern didn't.

"I don't repeat myself," Halvern said.

Dane met his gaze. "No. You don't."

He paused, then added, "But you also don't commit without understanding what you're stepping into."

That was the line.

The second man glanced at Halvern. Halvern's expression didn't change, but something in his attention sharpened.

"Then explain it," he said.

Dane turned slightly, angling his view toward the ground behind the structures.

"Settlement reports don't match physical output," he said. "Supply records are controlled. Equipment logs are consistent with underperformance—but not failure."

Halvern listened without interrupting.

"That suggests interference," the second man said.

Dane shook his head slightly. "No. It suggests limitation."

Halvern's eyes narrowed slightly. "Continue."

Dane gestured lightly toward the ground.

"Readings show variance below surface level," he said. "Not stable enough to classify, not weak enough to dismiss."

Halvern said nothing.

"Which means?" the second man pressed.

Dane looked at him.

"It means no one closed the category."

That landed.

Halvern stepped forward—not toward Dane, but toward the ground—and stopped at the edge of the marked area. For a moment, no one spoke.

Then Halvern said, "Scan it."

The third man moved immediately, stepping forward with a more advanced unit than Graham had used. He ran the scan once, then again.

The device responded—imperfect, incomplete, but present.

The third man looked up. "Consistent with prior reading."

Halvern nodded once, then turned slightly, looking back at Dane.

"How long have you known?"

Dane didn't hesitate. "Long enough to know it matters."

Halvern held his gaze. "And long enough to act?"

Dane gave a slight shake of his head. "No. Not alone."

Another pause.

Halvern looked back at the ground, then at the structures, then back at Dane.

"Who else?"

Dane gave the same answer again. "Not many."

The second man shifted. "That's not acceptable."

Halvern raised a hand slightly. The man stopped.

Halvern didn't look at him. "Control is acceptable," he said quietly.

He looked at Dane again. "And that's what this becomes."

Dane didn't respond.

Halvern stepped back from the marked ground.

"We'll take over from here," he said.

There it was.

Dane let a moment pass.

"On what authority?" he asked.

The question wasn't defiant. It was necessary.

Halvern's expression didn't change. "The kind that doesn't require explanation."

Dane gave a small nod. "Then you won't mind putting it in writing."

The second man reacted immediately. "That's not how—"

Halvern stopped him again with a slight motion.

This time, he looked directly at Dane. For a long moment.

Then he said, "No. But I will define it."

Dane held his gaze. "That's a start."

Halvern turned toward his team.

"Prepare the site," he said.

The third man moved immediately. The second followed, already issuing quiet instructions.

Halvern paused once more.

"Mercer."

Dane waited.

"You'll remain," Halvern said.

Not a request.

Dane gave a slight nod. "Understood."

Halvern studied him one last time, then turned and walked back toward the craft—not leaving, but repositioning.

Dane stood still until the movement settled, then turned.

Inside, Alex looked up as he entered.

"Well?" she asked.

Dane exhaled slowly.

"They're in."

Marcus gave a faint smile. "No. They think they are."

Bill stepped forward.

"How far?"

Dane met his gaze. "Far enough."

He paused, then added, "They want control."

Marcus nodded. "Of course they do."

Dane looked back toward the open ground.

"And they're about to ask for it."

Chapter 16 — Terms of Control

They didn't ask for control immediately. That was the first sign they intended to keep it.

Halvern let the site settle under his presence. His team moved with quiet efficiency—equipment staged, perimeter loosely defined, access points observed without being formally established. They were not claiming the space. They were becoming part of it.

Inside, Alex watched the movement through the feed.

"They're setting structure," she said.

Joren nodded. "Soft perimeter. No declarations."

Marcus leaned back slightly. "They're waiting."

"For what?" Elias asked.

Marcus glanced toward the entrance. "For the moment they don't have to ask."

Dane stood near the opening, watching.

"They'll come back in," he said.

Bill stepped beside him. "Yes."

A brief pause followed.

"And when they do," Bill added, "we're ready."

It didn't take long.

Halvern entered without announcement. The second man followed. The third remained outside.

Dane didn't move to meet him this time. He let Halvern come to him.

"You were right," Halvern said.

Dane didn't answer.

Halvern glanced briefly toward the table where Alex's display rested. "Partially," he added.

Alex didn't look up. "Partial is enough."

Halvern's gaze shifted to her. "You're the one managing the data."

"Yes."

He studied her for a moment, then nodded once. "Good."

That was all.

He turned back to Dane.

"This site is no longer inactive," he said. "It falls under directed review."

Dane gave a slight nod. "Defined how?"

Halvern's expression didn't change. "By us."

There it was.

Dane let a moment pass, then stepped slightly aside.

"You'll want to sit," he said.

Halvern didn't move immediately. Then, after a brief pause, he did. The second man remained standing.

Alex shifted the display slightly but did not turn it toward them. Not yet.

Marcus remained seated in the background, quiet, watching.

Lillian stepped forward. She had not moved quickly or drawn attention, but now she was exactly where she needed to be.

"You said you would define it," she said.

Halvern looked at her. "I did."

"Then define it," Lillian replied.

The second man turned toward her. "Who are you?"

Lillian didn't look at him. "The one who understands what happens next."

Halvern's attention sharpened slightly. "Go on."

Lillian inclined her head slightly.

"You've identified potential value," she said. "Unverified, but enough to act."

Halvern didn't respond.

"You've initiated control," she continued, "without formal declaration."

A brief pause followed.

"That works for access," she said. "It doesn't work for ownership."

The second man stepped forward slightly. "That's not your concern."

Lillian looked at him then—calm, unmoved.

"It becomes my concern the moment you intend to take something that isn't yet defined."

Silence followed.

Halvern didn't interrupt.

That told her everything.

She continued.

"The current contract structure defines surface and operational control," she said. "It does not define reclassification of subsurface discovery."

Alex watched closely. No movement. No interruption.

Lillian stepped slightly closer to the table.

"If what you believe is here is real, then it does not fall under your existing authority."

The second man started to speak again, but Halvern stopped him.

"Explain," Halvern said.

Lillian nodded once.

"You can take the site. You can control access. You can restrict movement."

She paused.

"But you cannot claim what has not been classified under your structure."

Halvern leaned back slightly.

"And who defines that classification?"

Lillian met his gaze. "The one who closes the category."

There it was.

Marcus's faint smile returned.

Halvern considered her for a long moment.

"And that's you?" he asked.

Lillian didn't answer immediately.

"No," she said at last. "But it could be."

The room held still.

Halvern looked at her more carefully now.

"Say that again."

Lillian didn't move.

"You don't currently own what's here. You control the structure around it. This sits outside that structure."

Halvern's eyes narrowed slightly.

"And you're offering to bring it inside."

Lillian inclined her head. "For a price."

The second man stepped forward. "This isn't a negotiation—"

Halvern raised his hand again, stopping him.

"What price?" Halvern asked.

Dane remained still. Alex didn't move. Marcus watched.

Lillian answered.

"Defined authority," she said. Then, after a brief pause, "Documented."

Halvern considered that.

"You want recognition."

"No," Lillian replied. "I want structure."

Another pause followed.

"And what does that give me?" he asked.

"Control that holds," Lillian said.

Silence settled again.

Halvern looked at Dane, then back at Lillian.

"You're asking me to formalize something I already have."

Lillian shook her head slightly.

"No. I'm asking you to secure something you don't."

That was the shift.

Halvern saw it.

He leaned forward.

"Draft it," he said.

The second man turned sharply. "Director—"

Halvern didn't look at him. "Draft it," he repeated.

Lillian nodded once. "Then we'll define it properly."

Halvern stood.

"This moves quickly," he said.

Lillian met his gaze. "It has to."

He studied her one last time, then turned and left the structure. The second man followed, less certain now than before.

Outside, the movement resumed.

Inside, the room remained still for a moment longer.

Then Marcus said quietly, "There it is."

Alex looked at Lillian. "He agreed."

Lillian didn't smile. "He committed."

Bill stepped forward.

"How far did that move us?"

Lillian's answer was calm.

"Far enough that he can't step back cleanly."

Dane exhaled slowly.

"And now?"

Marcus leaned back slightly.

"Now," he said, "we write the trap."

Chapter 17 — The Draft

They didn't rush the document. That was the first decision.

Lillian sat at the table with the display angled slightly away from the room—not hidden, not exposed, just enough to signal that what she was doing mattered and required focus. Alex stood nearby, monitoring the incoming data streams without speaking. Joren remained at the secondary console, ensuring that everything feeding into the structure remained stable.

Marcus stayed where he always did—just outside the center of attention, watching everything. Dane leaned against the far side of the room, silent. Bill remained near the entrance.

No one interrupted.

Lillian began with the structure—not the language, not the terms, but the structure itself.

"Existing authority references surface and operational control," she said quietly, more to confirm than to explain.

Alex nodded. "Confirmed."

Lillian adjusted the framework.

"Subsurface classification remains undefined," she continued.

Joren added, "Consistent across all related contracts."

Lillian paused.

That was the opening.

She began building from there.

"Initial clause," she said. "Temporary classification authority granted for purposes of evaluation and containment."

Dane glanced toward her. "Temporary?"

Lillian didn't look up. "Yes."

Marcus gave a faint smile. "Good."

Alex understood immediately. "Temporary invites extension."

Lillian inclined her head slightly. "Yes."

She continued typing.

"Authority limited to defined scope," she said.

Joren nodded. "Scope defined how?"

"By the data," Lillian replied without hesitation.

Marcus's smile deepened slightly.

Dane watched her more carefully now.

"That keeps them inside the structure," he said.

"And binds them to it," Lillian replied.

She moved to the next section.

"Access control granted for purposes of verification, extraction, and classification," she said.

Alex glanced at the wording. "You included extraction."

"Yes."

She paused briefly.

"They'll expect it."

Marcus nodded once. "They'll require it."

Lillian continued.

"Extraction contingent on classification stability."

Joren looked up. "Define stability."

Lillian's hands paused for just a moment.

"Measured consistency over time," she said.

Alex leaned slightly closer. "That's not immediate."

"No."

Marcus gave a quiet exhale. "That's very good."

Dane shifted his weight slightly. "You're slowing them down."

"I'm controlling the pace," Lillian said.

There was a difference.

She moved to the next section.

"Reporting requirements."

Alex nodded. "They'll expect internal reporting."

"Not internal," Lillian said, adjusting the clause.

"Shared reporting."

Joren frowned slightly. "With who?"

"With us."

The room stilled.

Marcus leaned back. "There it is."

Dane's eyes moved from the display to Lillian. "They won't like that."

"They won't refuse it," Lillian said calmly.

Alex understood why. "It legitimizes the structure."

"Yes."

"And it keeps them from acting independently."

Marcus nodded. "They won't see it as restriction. They'll see it as coordination."

Lillian moved again.

"Final clause."

She paused.

This one mattered.

Alex stepped slightly closer. "What are you anchoring it to?"

Lillian didn't answer immediately.

"Reclassification threshold."

Joren looked up sharply. "That's the trigger."

"Yes."

Lillian completed the clause.

"Upon confirmation of stable classification, ownership structure subject to reevaluation under updated designation."

Silence followed.

Dane exhaled slowly. "Say that again."

Lillian didn't look up.

"It means they don't own it yet," she said. "And they don't get to decide when they do."

Marcus gave a quiet laugh. "That's the trap."

Bill stepped forward slightly. "Can they see it?"

Lillian shook her head. "No."

Alex added, "Not the way it's written."

Joren nodded. "It reads as standard adjustment."

Dane looked at the display again. "They'll sign this."

Lillian finally leaned back. "Yes."

A brief silence followed.

Then Marcus said, "Good."

Lillian turned the display slightly now—not fully, just enough.

"Review it."

Alex stepped in first, scanning quickly but thoroughly. "It holds."

Joren checked the structural integrity. "No conflicts."

Dane took a longer look. "They'll move fast once this is in place."

Bill nodded once. "That's what we want."

Marcus stood. "Then we give it to them."

Lillian saved the document—not with emphasis, not with ceremony, just a simple confirmation.

"It's ready."

Outside, movement continued.

Inside, everything had shifted.

They had not taken control.
They had defined it.

Chapter 18 — The Review

Halvern did not read it immediately. That was deliberate.

He let the document sit on the display while the rest of the room settled around him. His team continued their work outside the structure, movement steady and controlled, but he did not join them—not yet.

He stood near the table, hands resting lightly behind his back, looking at the document without opening it.

Across from him, Dane said nothing.

That mattered.

Halvern noticed who spoke—and who didn't.

After a moment, he stepped forward and activated the display. The document opened cleanly. No excess. No unnecessary structure. That, too, told him something.

He began reading—not quickly, not slowly, but precisely.

Inside the room, no one moved.

Alex monitored the feed, her attention divided now—half on the system, half on Halvern. Joren remained still at the secondary console. Marcus watched without watching. Bill stood near the entrance. Lillian did not look at the display.

Halvern read the opening clause.

Temporary classification authority granted for purposes of evaluation and containment.

He paused, then read it again.

"Temporary," he said.

Dane didn't answer.

Halvern's eyes shifted slightly. "That limits scope."

Lillian spoke without looking up. "It defines it."

A brief pause followed.

Halvern continued reading.

Authority limited to defined scope.

His gaze shifted slightly.

"Defined by what?" he asked.

"By the data," Lillian replied.

Halvern's expression didn't change, but he noted it.

He moved on.

Access control granted for purposes of verification, extraction, and classification.

That line held his attention longer.

"Extraction," he said.

Dane answered this time. "You'll need it."

Halvern gave a small nod. "Yes."

He continued.

Extraction contingent on classification stability.

Another pause—longer this time.

"Define stability," he said.

"Measured consistency over time," Lillian replied.

Halvern leaned back slightly. "Time."

"Yes."

Silence followed.

Time was the only variable that mattered.

The longer Halvern believed he was refining the field…
the longer he remained exactly where they needed him.

Then he moved on.

Reporting requirements.

Shared reporting.

That stopped him—not abruptly, but clearly.

He read the clause again. Then once more.

"Shared," he said.

Shared reporting wasn't about collaboration.

It was about access.

Once systems were linked under that requirement, separation would no longer be clean.

"Yes," Lillian replied.

"With who?" Halvern asked.

"With those involved in defining classification."

Halvern's eyes shifted slightly. "That includes you."

"It includes structure," Lillian replied.

A pause.

Halvern considered that, then continued.

Final clause.

He read it once, then again—slower.

Upon confirmation of stable classification, ownership structure subject to reevaluation under updated designation.

Silence settled into the room.

This was the line.

Halvern did not react immediately. He read it again carefully, tracing the language—structure, designation, reevaluation.

Nothing incorrect. Nothing overtly restrictive. But not simple.

He leaned back slightly.

"You've left this open," he said.

Lillian didn't respond immediately. "Yes."

"Why?" Halvern asked.

Lillian looked at him now. "Because it is."

A pause.

Halvern held her gaze. "You're not defining ownership."

"No."

"You're delaying it."

"Yes."

Ownership delayed meant engagement extended.
And extended engagement meant deeper interaction—
the kind that required systems to speak to one another.
That was the opening.

Another pause.

Halvern looked back at the document, then at Dane, then back at Lillian.

"You expect me to accept uncertainty," he said.

Lillian's answer was calm. "I expect you to recognize it."

Silence followed.

Halvern did not move. He read the clause again—not for meaning, but for intent.

That was the difference.

Across the room, Marcus watched carefully. This was the moment—not the wording, but the interpretation.

Halvern stepped back from the table. Not rejecting. Considering.

"What happens," he said slowly, "if classification stabilizes in my favor?"

Lillian answered without hesitation. "Then the structure reflects that."

Halvern nodded once. "And if it doesn't?"

"Then it reflects that as well."

Another pause.

Halvern looked at the document one more time.

"You've made this adaptable," he said.

"Yes."

"Flexible."

"Yes."

"And controlled."

Lillian did not answer. She didn't need to.

Halvern understood.

That was enough.

He reached forward and closed the document—not dismissively, but decisively.

"It works," he said.

The room remained still.

Halvern looked at Dane. "You said this required structure."

"Yes."

Halvern gave a slight nod. "You were right."

He turned toward Lillian.

"Prepare it for execution," he said.

Lillian inclined her head slightly. "It already is."

That held.

Halvern allowed the smallest shift in expression, then turned toward the exit.

"Move forward," he said.

Outside, his team responded immediately.

Inside, the room remained quiet for a moment longer.

Then Marcus said, "He read it."

Alex nodded. "And?"

Marcus gave a faint smile. "He saw exactly what we needed him to see."

Bill stepped forward. "And nothing else?"

Marcus's answer was quiet. "Not yet."

Lillian closed the display.

"That's enough," she said.

Dane exhaled slowly. "He signed it in his head."

Marcus nodded. "And now… he acts on it."

And when he did, he would do exactly what they needed—
expand the scans, deepen the analysis,
and connect his system to theirs in ways the agreement now required.

Halvern believed he was moving closer to ownership.

He was moving deeper into exposure.

Chapter 19 — Execution Begins

They didn't wait. That was the first sign the structure had taken hold.

Halvern's team moved with purpose the moment the agreement settled into place. Equipment was repositioned, scans expanded, and the perimeter—once loose—began to tighten in ways that didn't require formal declaration. They weren't claiming the site. They were operating it.

Operating it—but only within the structure that had just been defined.

And that structure did more than permit action.

It controlled how fast that action could move.

Inside, Alex watched the shift unfold in real time.

"They've expanded their scan grid," she said. "Deeper pass. Wider range."

Joren checked the feed. "Still within the defined scope."

Marcus gave a faint nod. "They'll stay inside it. At least for now."

Dane stood near the entrance, observing the movement outside.

"They're moving faster than before," he said.

Bill stepped beside him. "Because now they think they're allowed to."

That was the difference. Before, every action had been cautious. Now, it was justified.

Outside, the third man adjusted a scanning unit, recalibrating its depth parameters. The device responded with a tighter signal, mapping the variance more precisely with each pass—not fully, not cleanly, but enough to reinforce belief.

"Signal consistency is improving," Alex said.

Joren glanced at her. "Because they're aligning with it."

Marcus's expression remained calm. "They're investing in it."

Elias frowned slightly. "Same thing?"

Marcus shook his head. "No. Alignment follows the data. Investment follows the expectation."

Expectation was the key.

The more Halvern believed something valuable was forming, the more time he would willingly spend confirming it.

Elias considered that, then nodded.

Outside, Halvern stood near the marked ground, watching as his team worked. He didn't give many instructions. He didn't need to.

That, too, was telling.

Dane stepped out to join him.

"Your team moves well," Dane said.

Halvern didn't look at him. "They should."

A brief pause followed.

"Progress?" Halvern asked.

Dane glanced toward the scanning unit. "Improving. Not stable."

Halvern nodded once. "Time will resolve that."

Dane didn't answer.

Halvern turned slightly. "You expected resistance?"

Dane met his gaze. "I expected uncertainty."

Halvern considered that. "And now?"

Dane gave a slight shrug. "Now you're committed to resolving it."

That landed.

Halvern's expression didn't change. "Yes."

Another pause.

Dane let the silence hold, then said, "Which means you'll want to accelerate."

Halvern looked at him. "Of course."

Dane nodded once. "That's where it gets difficult."

Halvern's attention sharpened slightly. "Explain."

Dane gestured toward the equipment. "Stability takes time. You push too fast, you disrupt the pattern."

Halvern didn't respond immediately. He looked back at the scanner, then at the data display one of his team members was monitoring.

"Then we don't push too fast," he said.

Dane held his gaze. "That's not how your operation works."

A brief pause followed.

Halvern's expression remained neutral. "No. But it is how this one will."

That was the shift.

**He had just done exactly what they needed.
He slowed himself.

Not because they told him to—
but because the system required it.**

Dane saw it.

Halvern had accepted the constraint.

And in doing so, he had accepted the structure.

Inside, Alex watched the exchange closely.

"He's adapting," she said.

Marcus nodded. "He has to."

Joren added, "He's adjusting his pacing to match the system."

Marcus gave a faint smile. "And the system belongs to us."

**Which meant every scan they ran,
every refinement they requested,
passed through a structure the settlement controlled.

The deeper Halvern pushed,
the more connected he became.**

Outside, the scan completed another cycle. The reading improved again—still incomplete, still unstable, but closer.

Halvern stepped toward the display.

"Report," he said.

The third man responded. "Signal integrity increasing. Pattern forming, but not consistent."

Halvern nodded. "Continue."

No hesitation. No reconsideration. Just forward movement.

Dane watched him for a moment longer, then said, "You're going to need extended access."

Halvern looked at him. "That's already defined."

Dane nodded. "Yes. Temporary."

A brief pause followed.

Halvern's eyes narrowed slightly. "For now."

Dane gave a faint smile. "For now."

That was enough.

Inside, Lillian reviewed the contract again—not for content, but for alignment. Everything was holding.

"They're operating within every clause," she said.

Alex nodded. "They haven't stepped outside it once."

Marcus leaned back slightly. "They won't. Not until they think they have to."

Bill looked toward the entrance. “And when they do?”

Marcus’s answer was quiet. “That’s when it tightens.”

Outside, the work continued—controlled, measured, committed.

They were no longer testing the system.

They were depending on it.

And they didn’t yet understand that it was guiding them.

They were no longer testing the system. They were depending on it.

And dependence required connection.

Each pass, each refinement, each adjustment— it all moved through the same controlled pathway.

The scans were not just revealing the site. They were opening access.

And Halvern, focused on what he might gain, had not yet considered what he was giving.

Chapter 20 — Pressure Builds

The first push came quietly. It didn't change the structure or break the pattern, but it increased the pace.

Alex saw it in the data before anyone said a word.

"He's tightening the cycle," she said.

Joren leaned in slightly. "Shortening intervals. They're running scans faster."

Marcus gave a faint nod. "That was coming."

Dane stood near the entrance, watching the movement outside.

"They're not waiting for stability," he said.

Bill stepped beside him. "They think they can force it."

That was the problem.

**Not because the scans would fail—
but because pressure forced repetition.

And repetition meant more data passing through the system.
More cycles.
More access.**

Outside, the scanning units began cycling more rapidly. The pauses between passes shortened, the recalibrations grew more aggressive, and the variance—once allowed to settle—was now being pressed. Not enough to break it, but enough to stress it.

"Signal consistency is fluctuating," Alex said.

Joren checked the readout. "It's still holding."

He paused, then added, "Barely."

Marcus didn't react. "Of course."

Elias frowned slightly. "That's not good."

Marcus shook his head. "No. It's necessary."

Elias looked at him. "Explain."

Marcus leaned forward slightly. "They have to push. If they don't, they lose momentum."

Alex added, "And if they push too far…"

Joren finished it. "They destabilize the pattern."

Silence settled into the room.

Dane turned back toward them. "So where's the line?"

Marcus's answer was simple. "Right where we need it."

Outside, Halvern stood closer to the scanning units now, watching—not passively, but actively.

"Run it again," he said.

The third man hesitated. "Cycle integrity is degrading."

Halvern didn't look at him. "Run it again."

The command wasn't sharp. It didn't need to be.

The scan restarted.

Inside, Alex's head came up slightly. "He did it again."

Joren nodded. "Pushing through instability."

Dane watched the feed. "That's not caution."

Marcus gave a faint smile. "No. That's investment."

**Investment kept him engaged.

Engaged systems stayed connected.

And connected systems could be observed—

and eventually, accessed.**

Bill glanced toward him. "Same distinction?"

Marcus nodded. "Yes."

Outside, the scan returned. The signal fluctuated, then settled, then shifted again—still not clean, still not stable, but stronger.

Halvern studied the result. "Better."

The third man didn't answer. He didn't agree, but he didn't argue.

That was enough.

Dane stepped forward. "You're accelerating."

Halvern turned slightly. "Yes."

Dane glanced at the equipment. "You risk destabilizing it."

Halvern's expression didn't change. "I risk losing it if I don't."

That was the truth.

Dane nodded once. "Then you'll want to manage the threshold."

Halvern looked at him. "Explain."

Dane gestured toward the scanning cycle. "You're increasing pressure. That works—up to a point."

Halvern waited.

"Beyond that point," Dane continued, "you don't get better data."

He paused.

"You get noise."

Halvern considered that, then looked back at the display.

"Where is that point?" he asked.

Dane didn't answer immediately.

That mattered.

Then he said, "Not fixed."

Halvern's eyes narrowed slightly. "Then how do you find it?"

Dane met his gaze. "You don't."

He paused.

"You stay just below it."

**Just below failure meant continuous operation. Continuous operation meant uninterrupted flow.

Exactly what the system required.**

Halvern studied him. "And you know where that is?"

Dane gave a slight shrug. "Closer than you do."

Silence followed—not tension, but assessment.

Halvern turned back to the scanner. "Adjust cycle timing."

The third man complied.

The next scan ran slower, more controlled. The signal stabilized—not completely, but enough.

Inside, Alex exhaled slightly. "He pulled back."

Joren nodded. "Just enough."

Marcus leaned back. "He's learning."

Learning the limits of the system—

without realizing the system was defining those limits for him.

Bill looked at him. "Is that good?"

Marcus's answer was quiet. "It's inevitable."

Outside, Halvern watched the stabilized reading, then said, "We push again."

The third man hesitated.

"Within limit," Halvern added.

That was the shift—not reckless, but controlled pressure.

Dane saw it and understood. "He's not going to break it."

Marcus nodded. "No. He's going to ride it."

Alex looked at the display. "And that keeps him inside the system."

**Inside meant connected.

And connection—sustained long enough—

would allow far more than scanning.**

Joren added, "Exactly where we need him."

Outside, the work continued—faster than before, more precise, more committed.

They were no longer testing the limits.

They were working within them.

And that made the structure stronger, not weaker.

Inside, Lillian reviewed the contract again—not for content, but for alignment.

"They're operating deeper inside the clauses," she said.

Alex nodded. "They're relying on them now."

Marcus gave a faint smile. "That's the pressure."

Bill looked toward the entrance. "And when it builds?"

Marcus's answer was simple. "They won't step out."

He paused, then added, "They'll go further in."

Outside, Halvern gave another quiet instruction. The cycle tightened again.

And the system held.

**Each cycle reinforced it.
Each adjustment deepened it.

Halvern believed he was refining the signal.

He was stabilizing the pathway.**

Tarsen didn't look at the primary display.

He didn't need to.

Everything he required was already broken down—patterns isolated, behavior mapped, outcomes projected.

"They've entered the cycle," one of the technicians said.

Tarsen gave a slight nod.

"Yes," he replied.

A pause.

"They believe they're controlling it," the technician added.

Tarsen's expression didn't change.

"They are," he said.

That answer settled into the room.

Not contradiction.

Clarification.

Across the secondary feed, Halvern's system ran cleanly—contained within the structure that had been built around it. Every adjustment, every push, every correction remained inside defined limits.

Not restricted.

Directed.

"How long once he commits?" another voice asked.

Tarsen stepped closer—not to examine the system, but to confirm timing.

"Thirty-six minutes," he said.

**Once Halvern committed fully to the cycle,
the system would remain open long enough.

Not forced.
Not breached.

Allowed.**

The room went quiet.

"Before detection?" the technician asked.

Tarsen nodded once.

"Before the system begins to recognize interference."

"And after that?"

Tarsen didn't answer immediately.

That mattered.

Then he said:

"After that, it won't matter what he recognizes."

Silence followed.

"He'll have already crossed it."

Crossed from control…
into exposure.

The technician looked back at the feed.

"And the data?"

Tarsen's gaze remained steady.

"We'll have what we need."

A pause.

"And he won't be able to take it back."

Another silence settled over the room.

"Begin when he's ready," someone said.

Tarsen gave a slight nod.

"He already is."

Chapter 21 — The Ask

The request didn't come immediately.

That would have been easier to manage.

Instead, it built.

Halvern didn't push outward. He pushed inward—tightening the operation, refining the cycles, reducing variation with deliberate precision. Each adjustment appeared controlled.

But the direction was clear.

He was preparing for something.

**Not blindly—
but with the precision of someone who understood what the data was becoming.

The move that followed wasn't forced.
It was chosen.**

Inside, Alex watched the feed closely.

"We're inside the window," she said quietly.

Joren didn't look up. "How much margin?"

"Still good," she said. "But it's narrowing."

Marcus gave a faint nod.

"He'll move before it closes."

Dane stood near the entrance, watching the movement outside.

"He won't ask until he thinks we need him to," he said.

Bill stepped beside him. "And when he does?"

Dane didn't look away.

"He won't expect resistance."

Outside, the scanning cycles continued.

Tighter now.

Faster.

Cleaner.

The fluctuations had narrowed. Instability wasn't gone—but it was being pressed down, forced into smaller margins.

It looked better.

It felt better.

That made it dangerous.

**Because it felt controlled.

And control—at this stage—
was exactly what a skilled operator would expect to have.**

Halvern stood at the central display, reviewing the latest results.

"Consistency is improving," the third man said.

Halvern didn't look up. "Not enough."

The second man stepped closer, voice lower this time. "We're approaching threshold conditions."

Halvern's jaw tightened slightly.

"Approaching isn't reaching," he said—sharper now.

A brief silence followed.

The third man hesitated. "If we push the cycle rate—"

Halvern turned, just enough to stop him.

"We're not forcing noise into structure," he said.

Another pause.

Then, quieter:

"We get there clean."

But the edge was there now.

Not spoken—but present.

He looked back to the display.

Then made the decision.

"Bring Mercer."

Inside, Dane was already moving.

He stepped out before the message reached him.

They met near the center of the site.

No delay.

No formality.

"We need extended access," Halvern said.

**He didn't ask out of uncertainty.

He asked because the structure, as defined, made expansion the next logical step.**

There it was.

Dane let the words settle.

"For what purpose?" he asked.

Halvern held his gaze.

"To accelerate classification."

Inside, Alex glanced at the timing feed.

"We just lost another two minutes," she said quietly.

Joren nodded. "He's pushing faster."

Marcus didn't look up.

"He has to."

**Any operator at this stage would.

The pattern demanded it.

The progress justified it.**

Outside, Dane gave a slow nod.

"That moves beyond the current scope."

"Yes."

"You're asking to expand authority."

"Yes."

No hesitation.

No adjustment.

Dane studied him.

The pace.

The posture.

The push behind the words.

"That changes the structure," he said.

Halvern stepped slightly closer.

"It completes it."

A pause.

Dane glanced toward the scanning units.

Then back.

"You're not there yet."

Halvern's eyes narrowed.

"We're close."

"Close isn't stable."

Silence.

Halvern took another step forward.

Then another.

Not aggressive—

but no longer neutral.

"Then we stabilize faster," he said.

There it was.

Not just pressure.

Intent.

Dane shook his head.

"That's not how this works."

Halvern's voice lowered.

"It is now."

Dane met his gaze.

"For you," he said.

A beat.

"Not for the system."

That landed.

Halvern didn't respond immediately.

But the stillness tightened.

"Then define the limit," Halvern said.

Inside, Alex checked the feed again.

"Margin's tightening," she said.

Joren added quietly, "He's accelerating the clock."

Marcus leaned back slightly.

"Let him."

Dane didn't answer right away.

That mattered.

Then he said:

"Extended access requires adjustment."

Halvern waited.

"Documented," Dane added.

Of course.

Halvern gave a slight nod.

"Then we adjust it."

Dane didn't move.

"Not directly."

A pause.

"Not yet."

Halvern's expression hardened.

"You're delaying."

"Yes."

**From Halvern's perspective, the delay was unnecessary.

From the system's perspective,
it was essential.**

"Why?"

Dane held his gaze.

"Because you're not stable."

The words landed clean.

Halvern's team shifted behind him.

One of them spoke—quiet, but urgent.

"We're losing time."

That line now lands differently.

Halvern didn't turn.

Another added, more cautiously, "The signal may not hold at this level."

Now Halvern moved.

Just slightly.

But enough.

"You're asking for more control," Dane continued, steady. "While still relying on the structure you have."

A brief pause.

"That tells me you need it."

Halvern's voice was tight now.

"Yes."

Dane nodded once.

"Then you don't change it."

Silence.

"You extend within it."

Halvern exhaled slowly.

"That's slower."

"Yes."

"But it holds."

Another pause.

Longer this time.

"And if I don't accept that?" Halvern asked.

Dane didn't hesitate.

"Then you risk losing everything you've built."

A beat.

Then, more directly:

"Push this the wrong way—and it collapses."

Inside, Alex looked up again.

"We're still inside the window," she said.

A pause.

"Barely."

That matters.

Halvern turned back to the display.

The data.

The progress.

The narrowing patterns.

Everything he had invested.

Everything that was almost—

but not yet—

his.

He stood there a moment longer.

Then turned back.

"What do you suggest?" he asked.

**Not surrender—
but recalibration.

He wasn't stepping back.
He was choosing the path that would hold.**

Inside, Marcus allowed himself the faintest smile.

"There it is."

Dane answered immediately.

"We adjust reporting thresholds."

Halvern listened.

"Extend operational cycles under current authority," Dane continued. "Increase access through continuity—not expansion."

Halvern considered it.

"That keeps it temporary."

"Yes."

"And controlled."

"Yes."

Another pause.

Halvern nodded once.

"Do it."

Dane gave a slight nod.

"Lillian will define it."

Of course.

Halvern turned away.

"Make it fast," he said.

But the edge hadn't left his voice.

Not entirely.

Dane watched him go.

Then turned back toward the structure.

Inside, Alex looked up.

"Well?"

Dane's answer was simple.

"He asked."

Marcus nodded.

"And?"

Dane allowed a faint smile.

"He agreed not to get it."

That was the shift.

Lillian stepped forward.

"Then we extend the structure."

Marcus shook his head slightly.

"No."

A pause.

"We tighten it."

Alex nodded.

"He's deeper now."

Joren added, "And relying on it more."

Bill looked toward the entrance.

"And the next step?"

Marcus's voice was quiet.

"He'll ask again."

A beat.

"And next time…"

He leaned back slightly.

"…he won't just ask."

A brief pause.

Then Marcus added, almost as an afterthought:

"And next time, we won't have as much time."

Outside, the operation continued.

Faster.

Sharper.

More committed.

They were no longer asking if the system worked.

They were asking how far it could go.

And step by step—

they were being led there.

And step by step—

they chose the path forward.

It was the correct path.

The stable path.

The only path that made sense.

And it led exactly where it was designed to.

Chapter 22 — The Cost

The next phase didn't look different.

That was the problem.

From the outside, the operation appeared stronger than before. The scan cycles were cleaner, the data more consistent, and the structure more defined. Progress was visible, measurable, and steady.

But it wasn't free.

**Every improvement required more input.
More input required more cycles.

And more cycles meant the system stayed active longer—exactly as designed.**

Inside, Alex adjusted the timing feed.

"We're losing time," she said quietly.

Joren glanced over. "How much?"

"More than we should be at this stage."

Marcus didn't look up.

"He's accelerating it."

Alex nodded.

"Yes."

She paused.

"And it's working."

That settled into the room.

Alex saw it first.

"They're reallocating resources," she said.

Joren checked the feed. "From where?"

She adjusted the display. "Secondary systems. Support layers."

Marcus gave a faint nod. "They're feeding the operation."

**Feeding it kept it stable.

And stability required continuity—
uninterrupted interaction with the system itself.**

Elias frowned slightly. "That's normal, isn't it?"

Marcus shook his head. "Not at this stage."

Elias looked at him. "Why not?"

"Because they don't know what they're feeding yet."

A brief silence followed.

Then Alex added, quieter:

"And they're burning time doing it."

Outside, Halvern's team had expanded their presence. Additional equipment had been brought forward, and the scanning units now operated in overlapping cycles. Each pass reinforced the last, tightening the pattern and refining the signal.

It looked efficient.

It looked controlled.

It looked like progress.

Dane stood near the entrance, watching.

"They're committing deeper," he said.

Bill stepped beside him. "At what cost?"

Dane didn't answer immediately.

"That's what we're about to find out."

Outside, the third man adjusted another unit, linking it into the existing scan array. The connection held, but only after a slight delay.

"Integration lag," Alex said.

Joren nodded. "They're pushing compatibility."

Marcus leaned back slightly. "They're stretching their own system."

**Stretching it didn't break it—
it extended it.

Extended systems stayed open.**

Elias looked at the display. "Is that a problem?"

Marcus's answer was calm. "Not yet."

A pause.

"But it will be."

Alex checked the timing again.

"We just lost another minute," she said.

No one reacted immediately.

That was the shift.

Outside, Halvern reviewed the updated readings.

"Consistency?" he asked.

"Improving," the third man said. "But we're compensating across multiple inputs."

Halvern glanced at the display. "Compensation introduces error."

"Yes," the man said. "But it also increases coverage."

Halvern considered that.

"Then we manage the error," he said.

**It was the correct call.

Imperfect data could be refined.
Lost opportunity could not.**

There it was again.

Forward movement.

Always forward.

Dane stepped out to join him.

"You're expanding the array," Dane said.

Halvern didn't look at him. "We need more data."

Dane nodded. "You're getting it."

"Not fast enough."

Inside, Alex glanced toward Marcus.

"He's pushing harder," she said.

Marcus gave a faint nod.

"He knows he doesn't have time to wait."

A brief pause.

Then Marcus added:

"And he doesn't know how little he has."

Not because the data was failing—

but because time was being consumed faster than it appeared.

Outside, Dane glanced at the additional units. "You're pulling from outside your standard allocation."

Halvern turned slightly.

"Yes."

Dane held his gaze. "That's not sustainable."

Halvern's expression didn't change. "It doesn't have to be."

That was the truth.

Dane nodded once.

"As long as it resolves before it matters," he said.

Halvern studied him.

"It will," he said.

Inside, Alex adjusted the feed again.

"They're rerouting energy," she said. "Support systems are dropping."

Joren checked the secondary channels. "Non-critical functions are being reduced."

Marcus gave a faint smile. "They're prioritizing."

**And prioritization meant focus—

fewer systems monitored,
fewer safeguards observed,
more reliance on the active process.**

Elias frowned. "Is that bad?"

Marcus shook his head. "It's expensive."

Elias looked at him. "In what way?"

Marcus's answer was simple.

"In ways they don't measure until it's too late."

A brief pause.

Then he added quietly:

"And in ways that cost time."

Outside, the scan cycles tightened again. The signal grew stronger, more defined, more consistent across passes.

Not perfect.

But convincing.

Halvern watched the results.

"Closer," he said.

The second man stepped forward. "We're within projection range."

Halvern nodded once.

"Then we continue."

No hesitation.

No reconsideration.

Just commitment.

Dane watched him for a moment longer.

"You're getting what you want," Dane said.

Halvern didn't respond.

Dane added, "But you're paying for it."

That landed.

Halvern turned slightly.

"Everything has a cost," he said.

Dane met his gaze. "Not always this early."

A brief pause followed.

Halvern looked back at the data.

"Early cost reduces later risk," he said.

Inside, Alex checked the feed again.

"Margin's shrinking," she said.

Now Marcus looked up.

"How much?"

She hesitated.

"Faster than expected."

That mattered.

Outside, Dane gave a faint nod.

"Sometimes."

Halvern didn't respond.

Inside, Lillian reviewed the updated structure.

"They're still within the contract," she said.

Alex nodded. "Every move."

Joren added, "They're using it to justify expansion."

Marcus leaned back slightly. "Exactly as expected."

Bill looked toward them. "And the cost?"

Marcus's answer was quiet.

"Accumulating."

Outside, another scan completed.

The signal held.

Stronger than before.

More stable.

More convincing.

Halvern stepped closer to the display.

"Projection?" he asked.

The third man adjusted the parameters.

"Within range," he said. "But not confirmed."

Halvern nodded.

"Then we push to confirmation."

**Confirmation required depth.

Depth required sustained access.

And sustained access was where exposure began to accumulate.**

Dane stepped forward slightly.

"That increases exposure," he said.

Halvern looked at him.

"It increases resolution."

Dane held his gaze.

"And the cost?"

Halvern didn't hesitate.

"Acceptable."

Inside, Alex let out a slow breath.

"He's spending everything," she said.

Marcus nodded.

"He thinks he can recover it."

**And under normal conditions, he would.

The calculation was sound.

The timing… was not.**

A pause.

Then Marcus added quietly:

"He can't."

Outside, the operation continued.

More resources.

More pressure.

More commitment.

They were building something now.

Not just data.

Not just structure.

Investment.

And investment had weight.

Inside, Bill stepped forward.

"How far does he go?" he asked.

Marcus's answer was calm.

"As far as it takes."

A pause.

"And a little further."

Alex looked back at the display.

"They're locking themselves in," she said.

Joren nodded. "Every cycle."

Lillian closed the contract view.

"That's the cost," she said.

Dane stood at the entrance, watching the movement outside.

"They won't step back," he said.

Marcus shook his head.

"No."

A pause.

"They can't."

Then, almost quietly:

"And by the time they realize it…"

He didn't finish.

He didn't need to.

Outside, Halvern gave another quiet instruction.

The array expanded again.

And the system accepted it.

For now.

And the system accepted it.

Each expansion deepened the connection. Each cycle extended the interaction.

The cost wasn't just what they were spending—

it was how long they remained inside.

For now.

Chapter 23 — The Strain

The first signs were easy to miss.

That was what made them dangerous.

Nothing failed. Nothing stopped. The system continued to operate as expected—cycles running, data flowing, structure holding.

But the pattern changed.

**Not because the system was failing—
but because it was being asked to do more.

And more required correction.**

Inside, Alex adjusted the timing feed again.

"We're dropping faster now," she said.

Joren glanced over. "How much?"

She hesitated.

"More than projection."

That mattered.

Alex saw it before the others.

"The variance isn't settling the same way," she said.

Joren leaned in, scanning the feed more closely.

"Show me."

She adjusted the display, isolating the last three cycles.

"It's still stabilizing," she said. "But not consistently."

Joren studied it.

"Drift," he said.

**Drift wasn't loss of control.

It was the cost of maintaining it under load.**

Marcus gave a faint nod from the back of the room.

"Of course."

Elias frowned slightly.

"That doesn't sound good."

Marcus shook his head.

"It's not bad," he said. "It's pressure."

Elias looked at him.

"Same thing?"

Marcus's answer was calm.

"No. Pressure becomes bad when it's ignored."

A brief pause.

Then Marcus added quietly:

"And it costs time."

That line lands differently now.

Outside, the scan array continued its work. Additional units had been integrated, each feeding into the pattern, each adding weight to the system.

It held.

But it held differently now.

Dane stood at the entrance, watching.

"They've gone deeper," he said.

Bill stepped beside him.

"How far?"

Dane didn't answer immediately.

"Far enough to feel it."

Inside, Alex checked the timing again.

"We're inside the window," she said.

A pause.

"But we're compressing it."

Joren nodded.

"He's accelerating the system faster than expected."

Marcus leaned forward slightly.

"He's not waiting anymore."

That was the shift.

Outside, the third man paused over his display.

"Signal inconsistency," he said.

Halvern didn't look at him.

"Define it."

The man adjusted the readout.

"Pattern drift between cycles. Not large, but increasing."

Halvern stepped closer.

"Cause?"

The man hesitated.

"System load," he said. "Multiple inputs. Timing overlap."

Halvern considered that.

"Can you correct it?"

"Yes."

"Do it."

No hesitation.

No delay.

Just adjustment.

Inside, Alex saw the change immediately.

"He's compensating," she said.

Joren nodded.

"Trying to pull it back into alignment."

Marcus leaned forward slightly.

"That will work," he said.

**It was the correct response.

Compensation would stabilize the pattern—
but only by increasing the work required to hold it there.**

Elias looked at him.

"For how long?"

Marcus didn't answer right away.

Then:

"Less time than he thinks."

That matters.

Outside, the next cycle ran.

The drift reduced.

Not eliminated.

But controlled.

Halvern watched the result.

"Better," he said.

The third man didn't respond.

He was already adjusting the next pass.

Dane stepped forward.

"You're seeing instability," he said.

Halvern turned slightly.

"Yes."

Dane gestured toward the array.

"You're pushing the system harder than it was designed for."

Halvern's expression didn't change.

"Then we redesign it."

Dane held his gaze.

"That's not immediate."

"No."

Halvern turned back to the display.

"But it's necessary."

There it was again.

Commitment.

Inside, Alex glanced at the timing feed.

"We just lost another minute," she said.

No one responded immediately.

Now it's becoming normal.

Dane nodded once.

"And until then?" he asked.

Halvern didn't look at him.

"We manage it."

And managing it meant staying engaged—cycle after cycle, adjustment after adjustment.

Inside, Alex adjusted the feed again.

"They're layering corrections," she said.

Joren checked the pattern.

"Each cycle is compensating for the last."

Marcus gave a faint smile.

"They're chasing stability," he said.

And each correction brought them closer—but required them to stay in the system longer to achieve it.

Elias frowned.

"And that's bad?"

Marcus shook his head.

"It's expensive," he said.

A pause.

"And fragile."

Then, quieter:

"And it's costing them time."

Outside, another cycle completed.

The signal held.

Then shifted.

Then held again.

Halvern watched it.

"Projection?" he asked.

The third man adjusted the parameters.

"Within range," he said. "But variance remains."

Halvern nodded.

"Then we refine."

Dane stepped closer.

"You're narrowing tolerance," he said.

"Yes."

"That increases sensitivity."

"Yes."

Dane paused.

"And risk."

Halvern didn't hesitate.

"Acceptable."

Because the alternative—

stepping back—

would mean losing everything already gained.

Inside, Alex checked again.

"Margin's getting tight," she said.

Now Marcus looked up.

"How tight?"

She hesitated again.

"Tighter than we planned for this stage."

That matters.

Marcus leaned back slowly.

"Good."

**Not because the system was weakening—

but because the pace was increasing.

And pace was what defined the window.**

Bill glanced toward him.

"Good?"

Marcus nodded.

"He's committing faster."

A pause.

"And we're still inside the window."

That reinforces control.

Outside, the array adjusted again.

More precision.

More pressure.

More control.

The drift reduced further.

But not completely.

Never completely.

Halvern stepped back from the display.

"Maintain this range," he said.

The third man nodded.

"For how long?" he asked.

Halvern didn't answer immediately.

Then:

"Until it holds."

**A moving target.

One that required continuous correction to reach—and continuous time to maintain.**

Dane watched him.

"That's not a fixed point," he said.

Halvern glanced at him.

"No."

A pause.

"It's not."

Inside, Lillian reviewed the contract again.

"They're still inside it," she said.

Alex nodded.

"Every correction is justified."

Joren added, "They're using the structure to support the strain."

Marcus gave a faint smile.

"Exactly."

Bill looked toward the entrance.

"And when the strain increases?"

Marcus's answer was calm.

"They won't reduce it."

A pause.

"They'll compensate again."

Then he added, almost quietly:

"And they'll spend what little time they have left doing it."

Outside, the next cycle ran.

The signal held.

Barely.

But it held.

And that was enough.

Inside, Dane remained at the entrance, watching.

"They feel it now," he said.

Marcus nodded.

"Yes."

A brief silence followed.

"Do they understand it?" Bill asked.

Marcus's answer was simple.

"No."

A pause.

"Not yet."

Outside, Halvern gave another quiet instruction.

The array tightened again.

And the system responded.

Each correction kept it alive.

Each adjustment kept it active.

The strain wasn't breaking the system—

it was extending it.

For now.

Chapter 24 — The Edge

The change came faster this time.

There was no gradual shift, no slow buildup.

The system reached the edge—and stayed there.

**Not because it couldn't move further—
but because moving further would break it.

Holding it there required constant control.**

Inside, Alex checked the timing feed.

"We're getting close," she said.

Joren didn't need to ask what that meant.

"How much?"

She hesitated.

"Less than we planned for this point."

That mattered.

Alex saw it in the first cycle.

"It's not settling," she said.

Joren leaned in immediately. "Show me."

She isolated the latest pass. The signal formed, stabilized briefly, then wavered without fully resolving.

"It's holding," she said. "But it's not locking."

Joren studied the pattern.

"It's riding the threshold."

Marcus gave a faint nod from across the room.

"That's the edge."

**The point where stability no longer held itself—

and had to be maintained, moment by moment.**

Elias frowned. "That doesn't sound good."

Marcus didn't look at him.

"It's not bad," he said quietly.

A pause.

"It's dangerous."

Then he added, almost quietly:

"And it's costing us time."

Outside, the scan array operated at full capacity. Every unit was active, every cycle overlapping, every correction feeding into the next.

Nothing idle.

Nothing wasted.

The system wasn't just working.

It was being driven.

Dane stood at the entrance, watching the movement.

"They're all in," he said.

Bill stepped beside him. "No room left."

Dane didn't answer.

There was nothing to add.

Inside, Alex glanced at the feed again.

"Margin's nearly gone," she said.

Joren nodded slowly.

"He's running it right up against the limit."

Marcus leaned forward slightly.

"He has to."

Because stepping back would mean losing everything already gained. And holding position required continuous interaction with the system.

That was the truth.

Outside, the third man checked his display again.

"Cycle integrity is unstable," he said.

Halvern stepped closer. "Define unstable."

The man adjusted the data.

"Signal convergence incomplete. Variance holding across multiple inputs."

Halvern studied it.

"Is it collapsing?"

"No."

"Is it improving?"

A pause.

"Not consistently."

Halvern nodded once.

That was enough.

"Run it again," he said.

Inside, Alex's head lifted slightly.

"He's not pulling back."

Joren nodded. "He can't."

Marcus added quietly:

"He doesn't have time to."

That lands now.

Outside, the next cycle began.

Faster.

Tighter.

Pushed.

The signal formed again—sharper this time, more defined, but less stable. It flickered at the edges, struggling to hold its shape.

"Drift increasing," the third man said.

Halvern didn't respond.

"Compensate."

**Each correction held the pattern together—

but required another cycle to sustain it.**

The man adjusted the system.

Corrections layered over corrections.

Timing shifted.

Inputs rebalanced.

The signal steadied.

For a moment.

Then shifted again.

Inside, Alex checked the timing.

"We just lost another minute," she said.

No one reacted.

Now it's expected.

Dane stepped forward.

"You're overdriving it," he said.

Halvern turned slightly. "No. I'm holding it."

Dane met his gaze.

"That's not the same thing."

A brief silence followed.

Halvern looked back at the array.

"Then explain the difference."

Dane gestured toward the system.

"Driving it increases output," he said.

A pause.

"Holding it increases strain."

**Strain didn't break the system immediately—

it kept it active longer.**

Halvern considered that. "And?"

Dane didn't hesitate.

"Strain breaks systems."

Halvern's expression didn't change.

"Not this one."

There it was.

Belief.

Not assumption.

Commitment.

Inside, Alex watched the pattern.

"It's slipping," she said.

Joren nodded. "Only at the edges."

Marcus leaned back slightly.

"That's where it matters."

Elias looked between them. "So what happens now?"

Marcus's answer was calm.

"They push through it."

Then, quieter:

"And they spend the rest of the window doing it."

That's a key escalation.

Outside, the system adjusted again.

More corrections.

More compensation.

More pressure.

The signal tightened.

Stronger.

Sharper.

Closer.

But not stable.

Never stable.

Halvern stepped closer to the display.

"Projection," he said.

The third man recalibrated.

"Within range, but convergence incomplete."

Halvern nodded. "How close?"

The man hesitated.

"Closer than before."

Halvern's gaze hardened slightly.

"That's not an answer."

The man adjusted again.

"Within measurable threshold."

Halvern studied the display.

That was enough.

He turned slightly.

"Push it."

Inside, Alex's eyes narrowed.

"There it is."

Joren nodded. "He's crossing it."

**Not past the edge—
but fully into it.

Where every cycle had to be maintained to keep it from failing.**

Marcus didn't move.

"He thinks he can."

Outside, the next cycle began.

Faster.

Harder.

No margin.

The signal formed.

Held.

Strained.

Then—

It nearly collapsed.

The fluctuation spiked sharply before stabilizing again under heavy correction.

“Integrity breach risk,” the third man said.

Halvern didn’t look at him.

“Hold it.”

**Holding required constant adjustment—

and constant adjustment meant the system could not close.**

The man adjusted rapidly, compensating across every input.

The system responded.

Barely.

But it held.

Inside, Alex checked the feed again.

“Margin’s almost gone,” she said.

This is the tightest point so far.

Dane stepped forward again.

“That’s the edge,” he said.

Halvern turned. “Yes.”

Dane held his gaze.

“You go past that, you lose it.”

A pause.

Halvern looked back at the signal.

Then said:

“Then we don’t go past it.”

That was the decision.

Not retreat.

Not escalation.

Control.

Inside, Marcus nodded slowly.

“He’s there.”

At the point where disengagement would cost more than continuation.

Alex exhaled slightly. “And holding it.”

Joren added, "For now."

Marcus added quietly:

"Not for long."

Outside, the system stabilized again.

Not fully.

Not cleanly.

But enough.

Halvern stepped back.

"Maintain this level," he said.

The third man nodded. "For how long?"

Halvern didn't answer immediately.

Then:

"Until it resolves."

Dane watched him.

"That's not guaranteed."

Halvern glanced at him. "No."

A pause.

"But it's necessary."

Inside, Lillian reviewed the contract again.

"They're still within bounds," she said.

Alex nodded. "Barely."

Marcus gave a faint smile.

"That's where we want them."

Bill looked toward the entrance.

"And the next move?"

Marcus's answer was quiet.

"He'll try to lock it in."

A pause.

"He'll want certainty."

Then, almost as an afterthought:

"And he won't have time to get it."

Outside, the system continued.

At the edge.

Balanced.

Strained.

Holding.

And everyone could feel it—

even if not all of them understood it.

And everyone could feel it—
even if not all of them understood it.

The system wasn't just running anymore. It was being held open.

And as long as it remained there—

it remained exposed.

Chapter 25 — The Lock

The shift came in the tone.

Not in the data.

Not in the system.

In him.

Halvern no longer studied the pattern to understand it. He studied it to confirm what he already believed.

That changed everything.

**Because decision replaced evaluation.

And once a decision was made,
it had to be carried through.**

Alex saw it in the way he moved.

"He's not analyzing anymore," she said quietly. "He's deciding."

Joren glanced at the feed. "Based on what?"

Alex didn't answer immediately.

"On what he thinks it is," she said.

Marcus gave a faint nod. "That's the moment."

**The point where confirmation mattered less than commitment—

and commitment required action.**

Dane stood at the entrance, watching Halvern near the central display.

"He's ready," Dane said.

**Not because the data was complete—

but because it was sufficient to justify the next step.**

Bill stepped beside him. "For what?"

Dane didn't look away. "To claim it."

Outside, the system held at the edge—strained, balanced, responsive under constant correction.

The signal remained consistent enough to support belief.

Not enough to prove.

But enough to justify action.

Halvern stepped closer to the display.

"Projection," he said.

The third man adjusted the readout.

"Convergence approaching threshold," he said. "Stability improving under controlled conditions."

Halvern nodded once.

That was all he needed.

He turned.

"Prepare to formalize classification," he said.

Formalization required the system to remain active—continuous, uninterrupted, and fully engaged.

There it was.

Inside, Alex's head lifted.

"He's moving," she said.

Joren nodded. "He wants to lock it."

Marcus leaned forward slightly. "Of course he does."

Bill looked toward them. "Can he?"

Marcus's answer was calm. "Not yet."

Outside, Dane stepped forward.

"You're ahead of your data," he said.

Halvern turned slightly.

"No," he said. "I'm ahead of your hesitation."

Dane met his gaze.

"That's not the same thing."

A brief silence followed.

Halvern stepped closer.

"You said it would resolve," he said.

Dane nodded. "I said it would stabilize."

Halvern's eyes narrowed.

"And it has."

Dane shook his head slightly.

"It's holding," he said. "That's different."

Halvern studied him.

"You're drawing a distinction that doesn't matter."

Dane didn't move.

"It matters if you're about to act on it."

A pause followed.

Halvern looked back at the display.

The signal held.

Strained.

Balanced.

Convincing.

He turned again.

"Define the difference," he said.

Dane answered without hesitation.

"Stability holds under pressure," he said.

A pause.

"This holds because of it."

Halvern considered that.

"And?"

Dane met his gaze.

"Remove the pressure," he said, "and you don't know what you have."

Silence followed.

Halvern didn't respond immediately.

He looked at the system again.

The cycles.

The corrections.

The constant input.

He understood.

But not enough.

"Then we don't remove it," he said.

**Because removing pressure would undo the progress—

and maintaining it meant the system could not close.**

There it was.

The decision.

Inside, Marcus gave a faint smile.

"He's locking himself in," he said.

**Not by mistake—

but by committing to the only path that would preserve what he had built.**

Alex nodded. "Completely."

Outside, Halvern stepped back.

"Begin classification protocol," he said.

The second man hesitated.

"Without full stability?" he asked.

Halvern didn't look at him.

"With sufficient confidence."

The man nodded.

That was enough.

Dane stepped forward again.

"You're formalizing under temporary authority," he said.

Halvern turned.

"Yes."

Dane held his gaze.

"That binds your claim to the current structure."

Halvern's expression didn't change.

"Then the structure holds."

Dane gave a slight nod.

"As long as the classification does."

A pause followed.

Halvern studied him.

"You're still delaying," he said.

Dane shook his head.

"No," he said.

"I'm defining."

Halvern looked back at the display.

The signal remained.

Consistent enough.

Strong enough.

Just enough.

He turned again.

"Proceed," he said.

Inside, Lillian stepped forward.

"Then we finalize the extension," she said.

Alex glanced at her.

"He's committing to classification under the current terms."

Lillian nodded. "Exactly."

Joren checked the structure.

"That locks every clause into place."

**And binds the operation to continuous execution—

until the process completes.**

Marcus leaned back slightly.

"And tightens them."

Bill looked between them.

"And after that?"

Marcus's answer was quiet.

"There is no after that."

**Because once initiated,

the sequence had to run to completion—

or collapse entirely.**

Outside, the system continued.

At the edge.

Under pressure.

Held together by constant correction.

And now—

Defined.

Halvern stood near the display, watching the classification process begin.

Data aligned.

Thresholds marked.

Structure applied.

It looked complete.

It felt real.

It wasn't.

Dane watched him for a moment longer.

Then turned back toward the structure.

Inside, Alex looked up.

"He's doing it," she said.

Joren nodded.

"Full classification attempt."

Lillian's voice remained calm.

"Under our terms."

Marcus gave a faint smile.

"And now," he said, "we close it."

Bill glanced toward the entrance.

"How?"

Marcus didn't look at him.

"We let him finish."

Outside, Halvern gave one final instruction.

"Lock the sequence," he said.

The system responded.

The classification process advanced.

And the structure held.

**The sequence could not pause.
It could not disengage.

It had to complete.**

And as long as it continued—

the system remained open.

Exactly as it was designed to.

Chapter 26 — The Turn

The change didn't happen all at once.

That would have been obvious.

Instead, it began as something small—something easy to dismiss.

A delay.

**Small enough to dismiss—

but large enough to repeat.**

Inside, Alex checked the timing feed.

"We're running short now," she said.

Joren looked over. "How short?"

She hesitated.

"Less than we need."

That mattered.

Outside, the classification sequence continued. Data aligned, thresholds marked, structure applied. The system responded as expected.

Almost.

Halvern saw it first.

"Why did that pause?" he asked.

The third man checked the display.

"Minor latency," he said. "System adjustment."

**The kind that appeared under load—

and stayed as long as the load remained.**

Halvern didn't respond immediately.

"Run it again," he said.

The sequence continued.

This time, it didn't pause.

But it didn't move cleanly either.

Inside, Alex watched the feed.

"There it is," she said quietly.

Joren leaned in. "Show me."

She isolated the sequence.

"It's not failing," she said. "It's hesitating."

**Not stopping—

but no longer moving cleanly through the sequence.**

Joren studied it.

"That's new."

Marcus gave a faint nod. "Yes."

Elias frowned. "That doesn't seem like much."

Marcus didn't look at him.

"It doesn't have to be."

Then he added quietly:

"And he doesn't have time to ignore it."

That line now lands hard.

Outside, Halvern stepped closer to the display.

"Report," he said.

The third man adjusted the readout.

"Sequence integrity holding," he said. "Minor timing inconsistencies."

Halvern's eyes narrowed slightly.

"Inconsistencies weren't present before."

"No," the man said. "But load has increased."

Halvern considered that.

"Compensate."

The man adjusted the system.

The sequence corrected.

For a moment.

Then paused again.

Short.

Subtle.

But there.

Halvern saw it.

He didn't speak right away.

Inside, Alex exhaled slightly.

"He's noticing it," she said.

Joren nodded. "He has to."

Marcus leaned back.

"Not yet enough," he said.

Bill glanced toward him. "What does that mean?"

Marcus's answer was calm.

"He sees the effect."

A pause.

"Not the cause."

**Because the cause wasn't a single point—

it was everything that had been layered into the system up to this moment.**

Inside, Alex glanced at the timing feed again.

"We just lost another minute," she said.

Now it matters more.

Outside, the sequence continued.

The pauses didn't increase.

They didn't escalate.

They remained small.

Controlled.

Contained.

But they were no longer absent.

Halvern stepped back slightly.

"Explain it," he said.

The third man hesitated.

"System strain," he said. "Multiple inputs. Overlapping corrections."

Halvern didn't look convinced.

"It held under that before."

"Yes," the man said. "At lower intensity."

Halvern looked back at the display.

The data still aligned.

The signal still held.

The classification process still advanced.

Everything worked.

Just not cleanly.

Dane stepped forward.

"You're seeing resistance," he said.

Halvern turned.

"No," he said.

"Not resistance."

Dane met his gaze. "Then what?"

A brief pause.

Halvern looked back at the system.

"Friction," he said.

**Not resistance from outside—

but the result of everything already inside the system.**

Dane gave a slight nod.

"That's one way to describe it."

Halvern studied him.

"You expected this."

Dane didn't answer immediately.

That mattered.

Then he said:

"I expected pressure to show."

Halvern's eyes narrowed slightly.

"And this is that?"

Dane nodded. "Yes."

A pause followed.

Halvern looked back at the sequence.

The delay appeared again.

Small.

Measured.

Repeatable.

"Can it be removed?" he asked.

The third man adjusted the system.

"Not without reducing load."

Halvern didn't respond.

Reducing load meant slowing down.

That was not what he wanted.

Inside, Alex watched the pattern.

"It's consistent," she said.

Joren nodded. "The delay is part of the cycle now."

**It wasn't introduced.

It emerged—from sustained correction and continuous load.**

Marcus gave a faint smile.

"That's important."

Elias looked at him. "Why?"

Marcus answered simply:

"Because it belongs."

Then he added, quieter:

"And there isn't enough time left to remove it."

That is the shift.

Outside, Halvern stepped closer again.

"Push through it," he said.

**Because removing it would require stepping back—
and stepping back would undo the progress.**

The third man hesitated.

"It may increase instability."

Halvern didn't look at him.

"Do it."

The sequence accelerated.

The delay didn't disappear.

It shifted.

Moved.

Changed position.

But remained.

Halvern saw it.

He didn't speak.

Dane stepped forward.

"You can't remove it," he said.

Halvern turned.

"Everything can be removed."

Dane shook his head.

"Not once it's part of the system."

A brief silence followed.

Halvern looked back at the display.

The classification continued.

Advancing.

Holding.

Working.

But not cleanly.

He understood that.

But not enough.

Inside, Alex watched the feed closely.

"He's pushing harder," she said.

Joren nodded.

"He thinks it's still controllable."

Marcus leaned back.

"He's testing it."

Bill looked toward him. "And?"

Marcus's answer was quiet.

"He's about to learn."

Outside, the sequence reached another threshold.

The signal tightened.

The classification marker advanced.

Then—

A delay.

Longer this time.

Not failure.

But not smooth.

Inside, Alex checked again.

"Time's almost gone," she said.

Now it's real.

Halvern stepped forward.

"Why did that extend?" he asked.

The third man checked the system.

"Cumulative correction," he said. "The system is compensating across prior cycles."

Halvern didn't respond immediately.

That meant the past was affecting the present.

That mattered.

He looked back at the data.

Then at Dane.

"This builds," he said.

Dane nodded. "Yes."

A pause.

Halvern's gaze sharpened.

"And it doesn't reset."

**What had been built into the system—

stayed with it.**

Dane held his gaze.

"No."

That was the moment.

Small.

Quiet.

But real.

Halvern saw it.

Not fully.

Not clearly.

But enough to feel it.

Inside, Marcus leaned forward slightly.

"There," he said.

Alex nodded. "He felt that."

Joren added, "He's starting to question."

Bill looked between them. "Is that good?"

Marcus's answer was calm.

"It's necessary."

A brief pause.

Then Marcus added quietly:

"And he doesn't have time to recover from it."

Outside, Halvern turned back to the system.

"Continue," he said.

Not retreat.

Not stopping.

Forward.

But now—

aware.

Dane watched him for a moment longer.

Then turned back toward the structure.

Inside, Alex looked up.

"Well?" she asked.

Dane's answer was quiet.

"He noticed."

Marcus gave a faint smile.

"Good."

A pause.

"Now it gets interesting."

Outside, the sequence continued.

Holding.

Delaying.

Advancing.

And for the first time—

not fully trusted.

And for the first time—

not fully trusted.

But still required.

Because stopping now
would cost more
than continuing.

Chapter 27 — The Doubt

Halvern didn't stop the process.

That was the first decision.

He could have paused the sequence, reduced the load, reset the structure, and re-evaluated. It would have been the cautious approach—the controlled approach.

He didn't choose it.

**Because stepping back would cost him everything he had already built.

And moving forward—
was the only way to preserve it.**

Instead, he watched.

The sequence continued in front of him, advancing in measured steps. The data aligned, the signal held, and the classification markers moved forward.

But now he was no longer observing progress.

He was watching for error.

Inside, Alex glanced at the timing feed.

"We're almost out," she said.

Joren didn't ask how much.

He already knew what that meant.

Alex saw the shift.

"He's not tracking results anymore," she said. "He's tracking deviation."

Joren nodded. "Looking for cause."

Marcus leaned back slightly. "Good."

Elias frowned. "Good?"

Marcus didn't look at him.

"He needs a reason."

Because once doubt enters the system,
it has to be resolved—
or carried forward.

Then, quietly:

"And he doesn't have time to find the right one."

Outside, Halvern stepped closer to the display again.

"Run the last three cycles," he said.

The third man complied.

The sequence replayed—each cycle layered over the last, each showing the same pattern: formation, stabilization, delay.

Halvern watched carefully.

"Again," he said.

The replay ran again.

The delay appeared.

Small.

Precise.

Consistent.

Halvern's eyes narrowed.

"It's not random," he said.

**Which meant it could be understood—

but only if there was time to do so.**

"No," the third man replied. "It's consistent under load."

Halvern didn't answer.

Consistent meant predictable.

Predictable meant defined.

Defined meant—

Inside, Alex checked the feed again.

"Minutes now," she said.

No one responded.

They didn't need to.

Halvern turned slightly.

"What's introducing it?" he asked.

The third man hesitated.

"System interaction," he said. "Multiple inputs, overlapping corrections."

Halvern shook his head slightly.

"That's an effect," he said. "Not a cause."

**And finding the cause would require stepping outside the current cycle—

something he could no longer afford to do.**

A brief silence followed.

The man didn't respond.

He didn't have a better answer.

Dane stepped forward.

"You're looking for something outside the system," he said.

Halvern turned.

"I'm looking for something inside it," he replied.

Dane met his gaze.

"Then you won't find it that way."

Halvern studied him.

"Explain."

Dane gestured toward the display.

"You're treating it like failure," he said. "It's not."

Halvern didn't respond.

Dane continued.

"It's behavior."

A pause.

Halvern looked back at the sequence.

The delay appeared again.

Exactly where it had before.

"Behavior implies intent," he said.

Dane shook his head.

"No," he said. "It implies response."

Halvern considered that.

"To what?"

Dane didn't answer immediately.

That mattered.

Then he said:

"To pressure."

**Pressure he had chosen—

and now had to maintain.**

Inside, Alex watched closely.

"He's narrowing it," she said.

Joren nodded. "He's isolating variables."

Marcus gave a faint smile.

"He's almost there."

Bill glanced toward him. "Almost where?"

Marcus's answer was calm.

"Almost wrong."

**Not incorrect—

but incomplete.

And incomplete conclusions cost time to correct.**

Outside, Halvern adjusted the parameters himself this time.

"Reduce input overlap," he said.

The third man complied.

The next cycle ran.

Slower.

Cleaner.

The delay reduced.

Not gone.

But smaller.

Halvern watched.

“Again,” he said.

The cycle repeated.

The delay remained.

Different position.

Same presence.

Halvern stepped back.

“It moves,” he said.

“Yes,” the third man replied. “With system load.”

Halvern didn’t respond.

He looked at Dane.

“You knew this,” he said.

Dane didn’t answer right away.

Then:

“I expected it.”

A pause.

Halvern’s gaze sharpened.

“And didn’t say anything.”

Dane held his gaze.

“You weren’t asking the right question.”

Silence followed.

Not tension.

Evaluation.

Halvern looked back at the display.

“What question?” he asked.

Dane didn't hesitate.

"Not what's causing it," he said.

A brief pause.

"What it means."

**Because meaning defined the next move—

and the next move had to happen immediately.**

Halvern considered that.

The sequence ran again.

The delay appeared.

Small.

Controlled.

Consistent.

"What does it mean?" he asked.

Dane answered simply.

"That you're at the limit."

Inside, Alex exhaled slightly.

"He said it."

Joren nodded. "Directly."

Marcus leaned forward.

"Now watch."

Outside, Halvern didn't respond immediately.

He looked at the system.

The data.

The pattern.

The delay.

Everything still worked.

Everything still advanced.

Nothing had failed.

But something had changed.

"You're saying this is as far as it goes," he said.

Dane shook his head slightly.

"No," he said.

"I'm saying this is as far as it goes cleanly."

A pause.

Halvern's eyes narrowed.

"And beyond that?"

Dane met his gaze.

"You don't know."

And there wasn't enough time left to find out safely.

Inside, Alex checked the feed again.

"It's almost gone," she said quietly.

That's the final warning.

Outside, Halvern turned back to the display.

The next cycle ran.

The delay appeared.

Again.

He watched it carefully.

Then said:

"Push it."

Because confirming the limit mattered more now than preserving stability.

Inside, Alex's head lifted.

"There it is."

Joren nodded. "He's testing it."

Marcus didn't move.

"He has to."

Outside, the system adjusted again.

Higher load.

Faster cycle.

More pressure.

The signal formed.

Held.

Delayed.

Longer this time.

Not failure.

But not clean.

Halvern watched.

"Again," he said.

The third man hesitated.

"Instability is increasing."

Halvern didn't look at him.

"Again."

The cycle repeated.

The delay extended.

Then corrected.

Then extended again.

Halvern stepped back slightly.

He understood now.

Not fully.

But enough.

Inside, Marcus leaned back.

"He sees it."

Alex nodded. "Not clearly."

Joren added, "But he feels it."

Bill looked between them.

"And now?"

Marcus's answer was quiet.

"Now he decides what matters more."

Then, softer:

"And he doesn't have time to decide carefully."

Outside, Halvern turned toward Dane.

"Does it break?" he asked.

**Not as a question of safety—

but as a calculation of risk.**

Dane didn't answer immediately.

That mattered.

Then he said:

"Not here."

A pause.

"Not yet."

Halvern held his gaze.

That was enough.

He turned back to the system.

"Continue," he said.

Not confident.

Not uncertain.

Committed.

Inside, Alex watched the sequence resume.

"He's staying in," she said.

Marcus nodded.

"Of course he is."

A brief silence followed.

Bill looked toward the entrance.

"And the doubt?"

Marcus's answer was calm.

"It doesn't stop him."

A pause.

"It just changes how he moves."

Outside, the sequence continued.

Working.

Holding.

Delaying.

Advancing.

And now—

questioned.

But still required.

Because stopping here would mean losing everything without understanding why.

Chapter 28 — The Commitment

Halvern didn't hesitate the next time.

That was the difference.

The delay appeared again—subtle, controlled, present—and this time he didn't question it, didn't isolate it, didn't try to explain it.

He accepted it.

**Because removing it would require stepping back—

and stepping back would cost him everything already gained.**

That changed everything.

Inside, Alex saw it immediately.

"He's not testing anymore," she said.

Joren glanced at the feed. "What is he doing?"

Alex didn't answer right away.

"Moving forward," she said.

Marcus gave a faint nod. "Yes."

Elias frowned. "Even with the delay?"

Marcus didn't look at him.

"Because of it," he said.

**The delay no longer blocked progress—

it defined how progress had to move.**

Then, quietly:

"He doesn't have time to do anything else."

That lands hard here.

Outside, the sequence continued under increased load. The signal formed, held, delayed, then advanced—each cycle reinforcing the last, each imperfection absorbed into the system rather than corrected.

It wasn't clean.

It wasn't stable.

But it was consistent.

That was enough.

**Consistency meant it could be relied on—
even if it wasn't understood.**

Halvern stepped closer to the display.

"Maintain current parameters," he said.

The third man hesitated.

"With instability present?"

Halvern didn't look at him.

"With continuity," he said.

**Because continuity preserved the sequence—
and the sequence had to complete.**

The man nodded.

That was enough.

Dane stepped forward.

"You're choosing to operate within it," he said.

Halvern turned slightly.

"Yes."

Dane held his gaze.

"Even without full stability."

A brief pause.

Halvern's answer was steady.

"Stability is not required."

There it was.

Inside, Marcus leaned back slightly.

"He's crossed it," he said.

**Not into failure—
but into full commitment under current conditions.**

Alex nodded. "Completely."

Outside, Halvern looked back at the system.

"It works," he said.

Dane didn't respond immediately.

Then:

"It holds."

Halvern glanced at him.

"That's enough."

Dane met his gaze.

"For now."

A pause followed.

Halvern didn't argue.

He didn't need to.

He had already decided.

Inside, Alex glanced briefly at the timing feed.

Then looked away.

That moment matters.

She didn't need it anymore.

Joren studied the feed.

"He's no longer trying to remove the delay," he said.

Alex nodded. "He's incorporating it."

**Not correcting the system—
but adapting to how it behaved.**

Marcus gave a faint smile.

"That's the commitment."

Elias looked between them.

"What does that mean?"

Marcus answered simply.

"It means he's building on it."

Then, quieter:

"And there's no time left to change direction."

Outside, the system adjusted again.

Not to eliminate the strain—

to accommodate it.

Cycle timing shifted.

Corrections aligned.

The delay remained.

But now it was expected.

Halvern watched the sequence.

"Projection," he said.

The third man adjusted the parameters.

"Convergence within operational threshold."

Halvern nodded once.

That was all he needed.

He turned toward Dane.

"We proceed to final classification," he said.

Because waiting for perfection would mean never completing the process.

There it was.

Dane didn't answer immediately.

That mattered.

Then he said:

"Under current conditions?"

Halvern held his gaze.

"Yes."

Dane nodded once.

"Then it's defined by them."

A brief pause.

Halvern didn't respond.

He didn't disagree.

He simply turned back to the system.

"Begin final sequence," he said.

Inside, Alex exhaled slowly.

"He's doing it."

Joren nodded. "Full commitment."

Marcus leaned forward slightly.

"And now it locks."

Bill looked toward him.

"What does that mean?"

Marcus's answer was calm.

"It means he can't step back."

Not without losing the entire sequence he had already built.

Outside, the final sequence began.

The system tightened.

The signal aligned.

The classification markers advanced.

The delay remained.

But it no longer interrupted.

It belonged.

**The system no longer resisted it—

it operated with it.**

Halvern watched the progression.

"Maintain pressure," he said.

The third man complied.

The system responded.

Holding.

Advancing.

Defining.

Dane stepped forward one last time.

"You understand what this means," he said.

Halvern turned.

"Yes."

Dane held his gaze.

"This becomes your result."

A pause.

Halvern nodded once.

"That's the point."

There it was.

No uncertainty.

No hesitation.

Ownership.

Inside, Lillian reviewed the contract again.

"He's operating fully within it," she said.

Alex nodded. "Every clause."

Joren added, "Every limitation."

Marcus gave a faint smile.

"And every consequence."

Bill looked between them.

"And now?"

Marcus's answer was quiet.

"Now we let it finish."

Outside, the system continued.

Tight.

Strained.

Committed.

The final sequence advanced.

And Halvern stood there, watching it—

certain.

Invested.

All in.

**Because at this point,
continuing was the only way forward.**

And stopping
would cost more
than finishing.

Inside, Dane turned back toward the structure.

"He's done," he said.

Marcus nodded.

"Yes."

A brief silence followed.

Then:

"Now we close it."

Chapter 29 — The Collapse Begins

The system didn't break.

Not immediately.

That would have been too obvious.

Instead, it continued—just as it had before. The sequence advanced, the signal held, and the classification markers moved forward in steady progression.

Everything worked.

Almost.

**Because everything that had been built into the system—

was still there.

And now it was beginning to show.**

Alex saw the shift first.

"It's slipping," she said quietly.

Joren leaned in. "Where?"

She isolated the latest cycle.

"The alignment," she said. "It's not matching the previous pass."

Joren studied it.

"It's close."

A pause.

"But not exact."

Marcus gave a faint nod.

"That's enough."

**Not to break it—

but to change how it resolved.**

Elias frowned. "Enough for what?"

Marcus didn't look at him.

"For it to start."

Outside, the final sequence continued.

Halvern stood near the display, watching the data resolve in real time. The signal appeared stable, the pattern consistent, and the classification process nearing completion.

It looked complete.

It felt complete.

It wasn't.

The third man adjusted the readout.

"Convergence holding," he said.

Halvern nodded once.

"Continue."

No hesitation.

No reconsideration.

Just forward movement.

Dane stepped forward.

"You're seeing divergence," he said.

Halvern turned slightly.

"No. Minor variation."

Dane held his gaze.

"It's increasing."

A brief pause followed.

Halvern looked back at the display.

The next cycle ran.

The signal formed.

Held.

Then shifted—slightly more than before.

He saw it.

But not enough.

"Compensate," he said.

**Because correction had always worked before—

and there was no time to try anything else.**

The third man adjusted the system.

Corrections layered over corrections.

The signal realigned.

For a moment.

Inside, Alex watched the pattern.

"He's covering it," she said.

**Holding the pattern together—

but carrying forward everything already inside it.**

Joren nodded. "Each correction is pulling it back."

Marcus leaned forward slightly.

"That won't hold."

Bill looked toward him. "How long?"

Marcus's answer was calm.

"Long enough."

A pause.

Then, quieter:

"He's already past the point where it could."

That's your final "time" line—indirect.

Outside, the sequence advanced again.

The classification marker moved forward.

Closer.

Near completion.

The system tightened.

The signal formed again.

Stronger.

Sharper.

Then—

It misaligned.

Not failure.

But not correct.

Halvern stepped closer.

"Why did that shift?" he asked.

The third man checked the system.

"Residual variance," he said. "Carryover from previous cycles."

Halvern's eyes narrowed slightly.

"That wasn't present before."

"No," the man said. "It's accumulating."

**Each cycle building on the last—

without reset, without separation.**

That mattered.

Halvern didn't respond immediately.

Accumulation meant progression.

Not reset.

Dane stepped forward.

"It builds," he said.

**Because nothing in the system was clearing—

only continuing.**

Halvern turned.

"Yes."

Dane met his gaze.

"And it doesn't correct cleanly."

A pause.

Halvern looked back at the system.

The next cycle ran.

The misalignment increased.

Slightly.

But measurably.

He saw it.

This time—

he knew.

"Run it again," he said.

The third man hesitated.

"Instability is increasing."

Halvern didn't look at him.

"Run it again."

**Because stopping now would end the sequence—

without completing it.**

The cycle repeated.

The signal formed.

Held.

Then shifted again.

Further.

Halvern stepped back slightly.

It wasn't random.

It wasn't noise.

It was moving.

Inside, Alex exhaled.

"He sees it now," she said.

Joren nodded. "He understands it."

Marcus leaned back.

"Not yet enough."

Outside, Halvern studied the data.

"Explain it," he said.

The third man adjusted the readout.

"Cumulative deviation," he said. "Each cycle is inheriting the previous variance."

Halvern didn't respond.

He didn't need to.

He understood what that meant.

Dane stepped forward.

"You can't isolate it anymore," he said.

Halvern turned.

"No."

A pause.

"I can't."

Not without undoing everything that had already been committed.

There it was.

The first admission.

Inside, Bill glanced toward Marcus.

"That's new," he said.

Marcus nodded.

"Yes."

A brief silence followed.

Outside, Halvern looked back at the system.

The sequence continued.

Advancing.

But no longer clean.

The classification marker moved forward again.

Closer.

Almost there.

But now—

wrong.

Not visibly.

Not obviously.

But enough.

Halvern saw it.

He didn't speak.

He didn't stop it.

He watched.

The third man looked at him.

"Do we continue?" he asked.

A pause.

Halvern didn't answer immediately.

Inside, Alex watched the moment.

"This is it," she said.

Joren nodded. "He decides now."

Marcus leaned forward slightly.

"And he already has."

Outside, Halvern spoke.

"Continue."

**Because completion still held value—

even if correctness no longer did.**

Not confident.

Not uncertain.

Committed.

The system advanced again.

The misalignment increased.

The classification marker reached its final stage.

And locked.

Halvern stared at the result.

It looked complete.

It read complete.

It wasn't.

He knew that.

Now—

he knew that.

Inside, Dane turned back toward the structure.

"He's there," he said.

Marcus nodded.

"Yes."

A pause.

"Too late."

Outside, Halvern didn't move.

The system continued to run.

The data continued to resolve.

But the pattern was no longer correct.

And it wouldn't correct.

Not anymore.

What had been built into the system—
could not be removed without stopping it.

And stopping it now
would cost more
than finishing it wrong.

Chapter 30 — The Realization

Halvern didn't speak at first.

He stood in front of the display, watching the completed classification settle into its final state. The system continued to run, the data continued to update, and the structure held exactly as it had been defined.

It looked complete.

It behaved complete.

But it wasn't correct.

**Because nothing in the sequence had failed—

it had simply resolved under the conditions it was given.**

He knew that now.

Not as a possibility.

As a fact.

Behind him, the third man adjusted the readout again, running verification across the final sequence.

"Rechecking alignment," he said.

Halvern didn't respond.

He was already ahead of that.

Inside, Alex watched the feed.

"He's not questioning anymore," she said quietly.

Joren leaned in.

"No," he said. "He's confirming."

Marcus gave a faint nod.

"That's the shift."

A pause.

Then, almost quietly:

"And it's exactly where he was led."

That's your first Tarsen imprint.

Outside, the verification cycle completed.

The result returned.

Consistent.

Incorrect.

The third man hesitated.

"Final output matches sequence," he said.

Halvern turned slightly.

"And the sequence?"

The man didn't answer immediately.

Then:

"Deviated."

**Not broken—

but carried forward from everything that had come before it.**

There it was.

Halvern looked back at the display.

The classification stood.

Defined.

Locked.

Wrong.

He stepped closer.

"Run a correction pass," he said.

The third man complied immediately.

The system adjusted.

Recalibrated.

Reprocessed the final sequence.

The result didn't change.

**Because correction operated within the same structure—

and the structure itself had not changed.**

Inside, Alex exhaled slowly.

"He's trying to fix it."

Joren nodded.

"He won't be able to."

Marcus leaned back slightly.

"Not anymore."

A pause.

Then:

"It was never meant to correct."

That's the second layer—quiet but powerful.

Outside, Halvern watched the second pass complete.

The same result.

The same misalignment.

He didn't speak.

He didn't move.

He understood what that meant.

Dane stepped forward.

"You can't reset it," he said.

Halvern turned.

"No."

A pause.

"I can't."

The words settled into the space between them.

Not frustration.

Not anger.

Recognition.

Inside, Bill glanced toward Marcus.

"That's it," he said.

Marcus nodded.

"Yes."

A brief silence followed.

Outside, Halvern looked back at the system.

"Roll it back," he said.

Searching for a point where the system had still been clean—knowing there might not be one.

The third man hesitated.

"To which cycle?"

Halvern didn't answer immediately.

That mattered.

There was no clear point.

No clean moment.

No stable reference.

He knew that.

"Prior to deviation," he said.

The man adjusted the system.

The rollback initiated.

The sequence reversed.

Cycle by cycle.

The delay remained.

The misalignment remained.

Nothing resolved.

The system stopped.

The result remained unchanged.

Halvern watched it.

"Explain it," he said.

The third man checked the data again.

"The deviation is embedded," he said. "Each cycle carries the previous one."

**Not added at a single point—

but accumulated across every cycle that remained active.**

Halvern didn't respond.

He didn't need to.

He had seen it.

But now—

he understood it.

Inside, Alex nodded slowly.

"He sees the accumulation."

Joren added, "And that it doesn't clear."

Marcus gave a faint smile.

"That's the design."

A pause.

Then, more precisely:

"It's how the structure was built to behave."

This reinforces authorship—without naming Tarsen directly.

Outside, Halvern stepped back.

"Run a fresh sequence," he said.

**Testing whether the behavior would repeat—

or reveal itself as condition-based.**

The third man hesitated.

"Under current conditions?"

"Yes."

The system reset.

As much as it could.

The sequence began again.

The signal formed.

Held.

Then—

delayed.

The same delay.

In the same pattern.

The system advanced.

And the misalignment returned.

Immediately.

**Because the conditions had not changed—

and the system responded exactly as it had before.**

Halvern watched it.

He didn't interrupt.

He didn't adjust.

He let it run.

Until it reached the same result.

Again.

He exhaled slowly.

Not in frustration.

In certainty.

Dane stepped forward.

"It doesn't clear," he said.

Halvern turned.

"No."

A pause.

"It doesn't."

Inside, Alex watched the repeat cycle.

"He tested it," she said.

Joren nodded. "And confirmed it."

Marcus leaned forward slightly.

"He knows now."

Outside, Halvern looked at the system.

Then at Dane.

"This was built into it," he said.

**Not as a failure—

but as a consequence of how the system processed sustained input.**

Dane didn't answer immediately.

That mattered.

Then he said:

"It's part of it."

A brief silence followed.

Halvern held his gaze.

"You knew."

Dane didn't deny it.

"I understood the structure," he said.

Halvern's eyes narrowed slightly.

"And let it run."

Dane met his gaze.

"You chose to proceed."

**And the system had followed that choice—

to its natural conclusion.*

There it was.

The final shift.

Halvern didn't respond.

He didn't argue.

He didn't need to.

He turned back to the system.

The classification remained.

Defined.

Locked.

Incorrect.

And irreversible.

Inside, Bill exhaled slowly.

"That's it," he said.

Marcus nodded.

"Yes."

A brief pause followed.

"And now?" Bill asked.

Marcus's answer was calm.

"Now it becomes real."

A pause.

Then, almost as an afterthought:

"And now it belongs to him."

That line is powerful—because it ties consequence to choice.

Outside, Halvern stood still for a moment longer.

Then said:

"Shut it down."

The third man complied.

The system powered down.

The display dimmed.

But the result remained.

Stored.

Recorded.

Permanent.

**Not because the system failed—

but because it completed.**

Halvern looked at it one last time.

Then turned away.

Not defeated.

Not uncertain.

But changed.

Inside, Dane stepped back from the entrance.

"He knows," he said.

Marcus nodded.

"Yes."

A brief silence followed.

"Too late," Dane added.

Marcus gave a faint smile.

"Exactly on time."

Chapter 31 — The Reveal

Halvern didn't leave immediately.

That was the first sign.

He stood just outside the now-darkened system, the display dim, the equipment powered down, the operation silent for the first time since it had begun.

He wasn't looking at the machines anymore.

He was thinking.

Inside, Alex watched him through the external feed.

"He's putting it together," she said quietly.

Joren nodded. "He has enough now."

Marcus leaned back slightly. "Yes."

A pause.

Then, quietly:

"Enough to see the structure behind it."

**Not as a trick—

but as a system that had been allowed to run exactly as designed.**

That's your first Tarsen layer.

Elias frowned. "Enough for what?"

Marcus didn't look at him.

"Enough to stop asking what happened," he said.

A pause.

"And start asking how."

Outside, Halvern turned slowly.

His gaze moved across the site—the scan array, the support units, the placement of equipment, the way the system had been allowed to grow.

Then—

he looked toward the structure.

Toward them.

Dane stepped out before he could be called.

They met in the open space between the system and the building.

For a moment, neither of them spoke.

Then Halvern said:

"You structured it."

**Every constraint, every boundary—

set before the first decision was made.**

Not a question.

A statement.

Dane didn't answer immediately.

That mattered.

Then:

"Yes."

A brief silence followed.

Halvern held his gaze.

"From the beginning."

Dane nodded once.

"From the moment you chose to engage."

Halvern's expression didn't change.

But something behind it did.

"You led me through it."

Again, not a question.

Dane didn't deny it.

"You made every decision," he said.
**And the system had simply followed them—
to their natural conclusion.**
Halvern considered that.
"Within the structure you defined."
**A structure that did not restrict choice—
only shaped the outcome of it.**
"Yes."
A pause.
Halvern looked back at the system.
"The delay," he said.
"It was part of it."
Dane answered carefully.
"It became part of it."
**Because everything that remained in the system—
was carried forward.**
That distinction mattered.
Halvern saw it.
"You knew it would accumulate."
Dane didn't answer right away.
Then:
"I knew what would happen under pressure."
Halvern's eyes narrowed slightly.
"And you applied it."
Dane met his gaze.
"You applied it."
The pressure.
The pace.
The decision to continue.
Silence followed.

Not tension.

Recognition.

Inside, Alex watched closely.

"He's not angry," she said.

Joren nodded. "Not yet."

Marcus gave a faint smile. "He won't be."

Elias glanced toward him. "Why not?"

Marcus answered quietly.

"Because he can see it's clean."

A pause.

Then, more precisely:

"And because it was designed to be."

Clear.

Consistent.

And unavoidable once engaged.

That reinforces authorship.

Outside, Halvern stepped closer.

"The contract," he said.

Dane didn't respond.

Halvern continued.

"It kept me inside it."

"Yes."

"And everything I did—"

He paused.

"Was valid."

Dane nodded.

"Yes."

That was the point.

Halvern looked back at the system again.

"The classification stands."

"It does."

"And it's wrong."

**Not because it failed—

but because it completed under the conditions it was given.**

"Yes."

A brief pause.

Halvern exhaled slowly.

"You built a system that fails under pressure."

Dane shook his head slightly.

"No," he said.

"I built a system that reflects it."

What pressure reveals.

What decisions create.

What cannot be undone once carried through.

That landed.

Halvern understood.

Inside, Alex leaned back slightly.

"There it is," she said.

Joren nodded. "He sees it."

Marcus didn't move.

"He accepts it."

Outside, Halvern turned back.

"You gave me control," he said.

Dane answered simply.

"You asked for it."

Halvern studied him.

"And you knew I would."

Dane didn't deny it.

"Yes."

A longer silence followed.

Halvern looked toward the structure again.

"You have others involved."

Dane didn't respond.

Halvern didn't press.

He already knew.

"You needed witnesses," he said.

Dane said nothing.

That was enough.

Inside, Marcus's gaze didn't shift.

"They were always part of it," he said quietly.

That's your subtle widening—Tarsen's operation is bigger.

Outside, Halvern stepped back slightly.

"Everything holds," he said.

Dane nodded.

"Yes."

"And I'm bound to it."

**Because the structure didn't just guide the process—

it defined the result.**

"Yes."

A pause.

Halvern looked at him directly.

"Legally."

"Yes."

"And operationally."

"Yes."

Another pause.

Halvern exhaled once more.

Then said:

"Clean."

Inside, Bill let out a slow breath.

"He said it," he said.

Marcus nodded.

"That matters."

Outside, Halvern turned slightly away.

Then stopped.

"One question," he said.

Dane waited.

Halvern looked back at him.

"Why?"

The word hung there.

Not accusation.

Not anger.

A question.

Dane didn't answer immediately.

That mattered.

Then he said:

"Because of what you've done."

**This wasn't created for you—

it was built from what you've always done.**

Halvern didn't respond.

Dane continued.

"The people you've taken from," he said. "The systems you've stripped. The structures you've built to make it look legitimate."

A pause.

"This is what that looks like from the inside."

Silence followed.

Halvern held his gaze.

He didn't argue.

He didn't defend.

He understood.

Inside, Alex lowered her voice.

"That landed."

Joren nodded. "Yes."

Marcus leaned back slightly.

"He already knew."

Outside, Halvern looked back at the system one last time.

The darkened array.

The silent structure.

The completed classification.

Then he said:

"What happens now?"

Dane answered without hesitation.

"That depends on you."

A pause.

Halvern studied him.

Then nodded once.

Not agreement.

Not surrender.

Acknowledgment.

He turned and walked back toward his team.

Inside, Dane returned to the structure.

Alex looked up.

"Well?"

Dane's answer was quiet.

"He sees it."

Marcus nodded.

"And?"

Dane glanced back toward the site.

"He knows it holds."

A brief silence followed.

Then Marcus said:

"Good."

He stood.

A pause.

Then, almost quietly:

"We'll refine it."

That line sets up Sting 2.

"Now we finish it."

**Not by changing the outcome—
but by letting it stand.**

Exactly as it was produced.

Exactly as it was chosen.

Chapter 32 — The Consequence

The system was quiet.

That was the first thing Halvern noticed.

No cycles. No corrections. No hum of machinery pressing toward resolution. The array stood still, the work complete, the result locked in place.

Wrong.

He didn't look at it again.

He didn't need to.

He already knew.

Behind him, one of his men shifted slightly.

"Director… instructions?"

Halvern didn't answer.

Not immediately.

Because for the first time since arriving at the site, the problem in front of him wasn't the system.

It was what came next.

And that had already been set in motion—

long before the system powered down.

Inside, Alex watched him closely.

"He hasn't moved," she said.

Joren leaned in. "He's processing."

Marcus gave a faint nod.

"No. He's calculating."

Working through outcomes that were no longer his to control.

Outside, Halvern turned slowly.

"Shut it down," he said.

The order came sharper than before.

Final.

The third man moved quickly. Systems powered off fully now, not just idled. The last active processes died out, leaving the site silent.

Halvern stepped forward, closer to the display.

"Pull the sequence logs," he said.

"They're already stored," the second man replied.

"Then isolate them."

A pause.

"Off-network."

The man hesitated.

"Director, the classification—"

"I said isolate them."

The tone left no room for discussion.

Inside, Alex's eyes lifted.

"He's trying to contain it."

But the structure had never been designed to stop at the site.

Joren nodded. "Too late."

Marcus leaned back slightly.

"He knows that."

Outside, the team moved quickly, attempting to segment the data—copying, isolating, locking down local storage.

Halvern watched every movement.

"Cut outbound channels," he said.

The third man froze.

"They're already transmitting," he said.

Halvern turned.

"What?"

"Archive routing initiated automatically under classification protocol."

That landed.

Halvern stepped forward sharply.

"Stop it."

"We can't," the man said. "It's already distributed."

Because once the sequence completed,
the system followed its final instruction.

Halvern's jaw tightened.

"How far?"

The second man checked.

"Multiple nodes. Primary network… secondary… external relays."

Halvern didn't move.

Inside, Alex exhaled slowly.

"There it is."

Joren nodded.

"He sees it."

Outside, Halvern looked back at the darkened system.

Then toward the structure.

Toward Dane.

This time, when he stepped forward, it wasn't controlled.

It was direct.

"You built this to transmit," he said.

Not as an extension—
but as its conclusion.

Dane didn't answer immediately.

That mattered.

Then:

"You agreed to the structure."

Halvern's eyes hardened.

"You buried it inside the structure."

Dane held his gaze.

"You used the structure."

A brief silence followed.

Halvern stepped closer.

"You think this holds?"

Dane didn't move.

"It does."

Halvern let out a short breath—not a laugh, not disbelief, something sharper.

"You have no idea what this touches."

That was the shift.

Not anger.

Not yet.

Something deeper.

Inside, Marcus leaned forward slightly.

"There," he said quietly.

Alex glanced at him. "What?"

Marcus's voice was low.

"He's not thinking about us anymore."

He's thinking about who receives it.

Outside, Halvern turned back to his team.

"Full shutdown. Everything. Now."

The third man hesitated.

"Director, the archive—"

"Everything."

The order hit harder this time.

The team moved.

Power dropped across remaining systems. Consoles went dark. Active links terminated where they could be.

But the data was already gone.

Already moving.

Already seen.

Halvern stood still for a moment longer.

Then he spoke again.

"Prepare transport."

The second man looked up.

"Return route?"

Halvern didn't answer immediately.

That mattered.

Then:

"No."

The word was quiet.

Final.

A pause followed.

"Alternate destination," he said.

The man hesitated.

"Sir?"

Halvern turned toward him fully now.

"Somewhere off-grid. No registry. No trace."

The meaning settled over the team.

Inside, Bill frowned.

"He's not going back."

Marcus shook his head slightly.

"No."

"He's running."

Because the consequence had moved beyond him.

Outside, the third man spoke carefully.

"Director… if this has reached central—"

Halvern cut him off.

"It has."

Silence followed.

No one argued.

No one questioned it.

They all understood.

Halvern looked back once more at the system.

At the structure.

At the place where he had committed.

Then he said, quietly:

"You won't get away with this."

Even as he knew—
it already had.

This time, it wasn't directed at Dane alone.

It wasn't even directed at them.

It was directed at the outcome.

At what had been set in motion.

Dane didn't respond.

He didn't need to.

Halvern turned.

"Move."

The team followed immediately.

No hesitation now.

No delay.

They moved toward the transport.

Inside, Alex watched them go.

"He's leaving."

Joren nodded.

"Fast."

Marcus leaned back slightly.

"Not fast enough."

Outside, Halvern reached the transport ramp and stopped only once.

He turned back—not to the system, not to the site—but to Dane.

For a brief moment, their eyes met again.

And this time, there was no calculation left.

Only understanding.

"You don't know what you've done," Halvern said.

Dane answered quietly.

"Yes," he said.

"We do."

Halvern held his gaze for a second longer.

Then turned and boarded.

The ramp closed.

The engines engaged.

And the transport lifted—harder, faster than necessary.

Leaving the site behind.

Inside, silence settled over the room.

Alex looked at the empty field where the transport had been.

"He's gone."

Joren nodded.

"And he's not coming back."

Bill looked toward Marcus.

"So what happens now?"

Marcus gave a faint, steady smile.

"Now," he said, "it reaches the people he's been working for."

Exactly where it was meant to go.

A pause.

"And they won't be as patient as he was."

Dane remained at the entrance, watching the sky long after the ship had disappeared.

"He's afraid," Alex said quietly.

Marcus nodded.

"Yes."

Another pause.

"Good," he added.

"Now the real consequence begins."

Chapter 33 — The Fallout

The silence didn't last.

It never does.

Within the hour, the first confirmations began to return.

Alex was the one who saw it first.

"It's hitting," she said.

Right on schedule.

Joren moved beside her. "Where?"

She expanded the display, pulling in external feeds.

"Multiple systems," she said. "Financial networks… registry offices… settlement records."

Marcus leaned forward slightly.

"Show me Hearthridge."

Alex isolated the feed.

And there it was.

Records—once buried—now open.

Clear.

Unhidden.

Elias stepped closer.

"What am I looking at?" he asked.

Joren answered quietly.

"Ownership transfers," he said.

A pause.

"Reversed."

Outside, the colony had already begun to change.

Word spread faster than systems.

Faster than data.

People moved between structures, gathering in small groups, voices rising—not in panic, but in something else.

Relief.

Elias saw it through the open entryway.

"They know," he said.

Dane stood just behind him.

"They're starting to," he replied.

Inside, Alex continued scanning.

"It's not just here," she said. "Other settlements tied to the same network… they're updating too."

Marcus gave a faint nod.

"It's unwinding," he said.

Following the same pathways it had been built on.

Bill looked toward him.

"All of it?"

Marcus shook his head slightly.

"No," he said.

"Just the part he touched."

Outside, a small group approached the structure.

Elias recognized them immediately.

Elias Rowan was at the front, moving faster than the others, his expression tight—not with fear, but with something held in check.

Behind him were several from the colony—faces worn from months of uncertainty, now carrying something new.

He stopped just inside the entrance.

"What happened?" he asked.

Dane didn't answer immediately.

That mattered.

Then he said:

"Your records were wrong."

The system corrected them once it was forced to resolve completely.

A pause.

"They've been corrected."

Elias studied him.

"That's not possible," he said.

Alex turned the display slightly so he could see.

"It is now," she said.

Elias stepped closer.

He looked at the data.

Ownership lines.

Registry marks.

Debt structures.

All of it shifting.

"All liens invalid," Joren said quietly. "Filed under improper authority."

Elias didn't speak.

He kept reading.

Then—

"My land," he said.

Not a question.

A statement.

Alex nodded.

"It's yours," she said.

The words landed harder than anything else.

Behind him, one of the others stepped forward.

"And the rest of us?" she asked.

Joren adjusted the display again.

"Same," he said.

"Every property tied to the structure has been released."

A silence filled the room.

Not empty.

Full.

Elias let out a slow breath.

"I don't understand," he said.

Marcus answered from the back.

"You don't need to," he said.

A pause.

"You just need to know it holds."

Elias turned toward him.

"And it does?"

Marcus met his gaze.

"Yes."

Outside, more people gathered now.

Not waiting.

Watching.

Hope moving through them cautiously, like something that hadn't been allowed in for a long time.

Inside, Alex shifted the feed again.

"There's more," she said.

Joren looked at her.

"What?"

She pulled up a deeper layer of the archive.

"Internal routing," she said. "Transaction logs… authorization chains."

Marcus leaned forward slightly.

"Go on."

Alex isolated a sequence.

"This wasn't just local," she said.

Joren studied the data.

"No," he said quietly.

"It wasn't."

Elias looked between them.

"What does that mean?" he asked.

Marcus answered calmly.

"It means the man you saw here…"

A pause.

"…wasn't the one in control."

Just the one positioned to act.

That settled into the room.

Alex expanded the display.

Names.

Identifiers.

Routing paths.

One chain stood out.

Higher clearance.

Deeper authorization.

More control.

Joren pointed to it.

"This one," he said.

"Everything routes through here."

Elias frowned.

"Who is it?"

Alex zoomed in.

The name resolved slowly.

Not fully.

Partially masked.

But enough.

Directorate Authorization: Level Two Command

Beneath it, a designation.

Kessler Division Oversight

Marcus leaned back slightly.

"There he is," he said quietly.

The one behind the structure.

Bill looked toward him.

"That's the next one?"

Marcus nodded.

"Yes."

Elias looked at the name again.

"And he's bigger?"

Marcus's answer was simple.

"Much."

A brief silence followed.

Dane stepped forward.

"What else?" he asked.

Alex continued scanning.

"There are transfer records," she said. "Funds moved off-world. Resource extraction logs… undeclared shipments."

Joren added, "And suppression orders."

Elias turned.

"Suppression?"

Joren nodded.

"Complaints flagged and buried. Legal challenges dismissed before they were filed."

Elias's expression hardened slightly.

"So it wasn't just us."

"No," Marcus said.

"It never is."

Outside, the colony continued to gather.

The news spreading now.

Voices rising.

Not in fear.

Not in anger.

Something stronger.

Recognition.

Inside, Elias looked back at the display.

At the name.

At the chain above the man who had taken everything from them.

"He's still out there," he said.

Marcus nodded.

"Yes."

A pause.

"And now he knows this failed," Elias added.

Marcus's expression didn't change.

"Yes."

Elias looked toward Dane.

"So what happens next?"

Dane didn't answer immediately.

That mattered.

Then he said:

"We decide if we stop here."

The room went quiet.

Elias looked back at the display.

At the name.

At the system that had nearly taken everything.

Then he said:

"No."

It wasn't loud.

It didn't need to be.

Behind him, the others nodded.

Not all at once.

But enough.

Marcus gave a faint, approving smile.

"Good," he said.

Alex looked at the data one more time.

"He's already moving," she said quietly.

Joren glanced at her.

"How do you know?"

She pointed to the routing logs.

"Activity spike," she said. "As soon as the archive hit the network."

Marcus leaned forward slightly.

"He's covering," he said.

**Too late to contain—

only enough time to react.**

A pause.

"And preparing."

Bill folded his arms.

"For what?"

Marcus's answer was calm.

"For us."

Outside, the light had shifted.

The colony no longer looked abandoned.

It looked alive.

Inside, Dane turned toward the group.

"This isn't finished," he said.

Elias nodded.

"I know."

A brief silence followed.

Then Marcus said:

"It's just the next door."

And this time—they knew what waited behind it.

Chapter 34 — Closing the Door

The colony didn't return to normal.

It became something else.

Not immediately. Not all at once. But the change had begun, and everyone could feel it.

Structures that had stood quiet now showed signs of life. Doors remained open longer. Voices carried farther. People moved with purpose—not urgency, but direction.

It wasn't relief alone.

It was ownership.

Inside the central structure, the displays had dimmed. The feeds still ran, quietly confirming what had already been established. Records held. Transfers remained reversed. The system did not shift back.

It stayed.

Exactly as it had been forced to resolve.

Elias stood near the entrance, looking out across the settlement.

"It feels different," he said.

Dane stepped beside him.

"It is."

A pause.

Elias nodded slowly.

"I didn't think we'd see it again," he said.

Dane didn't answer.

He didn't need to.

Behind them, Alex continued scanning the final confirmations.

"No reversals," she said. "No challenges filed."

Joren glanced at her.

"They won't move quickly," he said. "Not after this."

Marcus leaned back slightly.

"They'll move carefully," he said.

They'd seen what happened when they didn't.

Bill folded his arms.

"Which means they'll move eventually."

Marcus nodded.

"Yes."

A brief silence followed.

Elias turned from the doorway.

"What about him?" he asked.

Marcus met his gaze.

"He won't come back," he said.

A pause.

"But someone will."

Elias nodded once.

"I figured."

Outside, a small group had gathered again—not uncertain this time, not waiting.

Working.

Repairs had begun on structures that had been left to wear down. Equipment was being moved back into use. Lines were being redrawn—not on paper, but in practice.

Elias watched them for a moment longer.

Then said:

"We'll hold it."

Dane looked at him.

"You'll have to."

Elias gave a slight, steady nod.

"We will."

Inside, Alex closed the last of the open feeds.

"That's it," she said. "Nothing left to verify."

Joren stepped back from the console.

"Then we're done here."

Marcus didn't move.

"Here," he said.

Bill glanced toward him.

"And not here?"

Marcus gave a faint smile.

"That depends on what we decide next."

Elias looked between them.

"You're not staying."

It wasn't a question.

Dane answered.

"No."

A pause.

"But we're not finished."

This had only been one structure.

Elias nodded.

"I didn't think so."

He stepped forward slightly.

"That name," he said. "Kessler."

Marcus's expression didn't change.

"Yes."

Elias held his gaze.

"If he's above this…"

A pause.

"Then he's the one we should be concerned about."

Marcus nodded.

"He is."

Silence settled again.

Not heavy.

Not uncertain.

Clear.

Elias exhaled slowly.

"Then when you go after him," he said, "you won't be alone."

Dane looked at him.

"That's not a small step."

Elias gave a faint, steady smile.

"Neither was this."

A brief pause followed.

Marcus inclined his head slightly.

"Good," he said.

Inside, the room began to settle.

Equipment powered down fully. Systems closed. The structure returned to its original purpose—simple, functional, no longer the center of something larger.

Alex stepped away from the console.

"That's strange," she said.

Joren glanced at her.

"What is?"

She looked around the room.

"It feels quiet."

Marcus gave a faint smile.

"That's because it is."

Outside, the wind moved across the open ground, carrying the sound of voices from the colony.

Not loud.

Not urgent.

Steady.

Dane stepped toward the entrance and stopped there for a moment.

Looking out.

Watching.

Then he turned back.

"We move in the morning," he said.

Bill nodded.

"Back to the estate?"

Dane shook his head slightly.

"First," he said, "we prepare."

Marcus gave a faint nod.

"Yes."

Elias looked between them.

"For him," he said.

Marcus's answer was simple.

"For what comes next."

A brief silence followed.

Then Elias stepped back toward the entrance.

"I'll see you out in the morning," he said.

Dane nodded.

Elias paused once more.

Then added:

"And thank you."

It wasn't formal.

It wasn't practiced.

It was real.

Dane met his gaze.

"You held," he said.

Elias gave a small, quiet nod.

Then he turned and walked out into the light.

Inside, the room emptied slowly.

Not rushed.

Not delayed.

Just finished.

Marcus remained where he was for a moment longer.

Then said:

"He'll rebuild it."

Alex glanced toward him.

"The colony?"

Marcus nodded.

"Yes."

A pause.

"And that matters."

Joren looked toward the darkened displays.

"And the next one?"

Marcus's expression remained calm.

"He won't make the same mistakes," he said.

And neither would the ones above him.

Bill folded his arms.

"Good," he said.

"Neither will we."

Dane stood at the entrance one last time.

Looking out over the colony.

Then, quietly:

"We closed this door."

Marcus stepped beside him.

"Yes."

A brief pause followed.

Then he added:

"Now we open the next one."

And this time—they knew exactly what it would take.

Epilogue — The Second Door Opens

The report did not arrive loudly.

It never would.

It entered the system the way everything important did—quietly, routed through channels designed to prioritize without drawing attention, marked only by the level of authority required to see it.

Kessler saw it immediately.

He didn't open it right away.

That, too, was deliberate.

The office around him remained still, the light controlled, the space ordered with the kind of precision that suggested nothing was left unattended. Outside the transparent wall, the distant structures of the station moved in slow, regulated motion.

Everything where it belonged.

Everything under control.

Then he opened the report.

He read it once.

Then again.

Slower.

Not because it was difficult to understand—but because he wanted to see exactly where it had gone wrong.

The classification held.

That was the first thing he confirmed.

The structure remained intact, the authority valid, the sequence complete.

But the result—

He paused there.

Incorrect.

Not obviously.

Not in a way that would be dismissed by systems or flagged by standard review.

But wrong.

Precisely wrong.

Kessler leaned back slightly in his chair.

"Halvern," he said quietly.

Not with anger.

With recognition.

He continued reading.

The chain of actions unfolded clearly. Initial contact. Escalation. Resource allocation. Contract acceptance. Sequence acceleration.

Every step aligned.

Every decision justified.

Every movement within the boundaries of authority.

Kessler closed the report.

Not abruptly.

Carefully.

Then opened a secondary file.

Authorization routing.

There it was.

His name.

His clearance.

His division.

Connected.

Not implicated.

But present.

He studied it for a moment.

Then nodded once.

"They reached up," he said.

Not by chance—
but by design.

The assistant standing at a respectful distance didn't respond immediately.

That was intentional.

Then:

"Yes, sir."

Kessler didn't look at him.

"Halvern is no longer in position," he said.

It wasn't a question.

"No, sir."

"Location?"

"Unknown."

Kessler considered that.

Then gave the smallest shake of his head.

"Not unknown," he said.

A pause.

"Unstable."

That distinction mattered.

He turned his attention back to the report.

"They didn't stop at the site," he said.

"No, sir."

"They transmitted."

"Yes, sir."

Kessler nodded once.

"Of course they did."

Silence settled into the room.

Not uncertainty.

Assessment.

He stood.

Moved to the window.

Looked out—not at anything specific, but at the system beyond it.

Ordered.

Structured.

Predictable.

Then he said:

"They wanted this seen."

The assistant didn't answer.

He didn't need to.

Kessler turned back.

"They wanted me to see it."

This wasn't leakage.

It was placement.

A brief pause followed.

Then:

"They succeeded."

He walked back to the desk.

Opened the report again.

This time, not to review the failure.

To study the design.

"The delay," he said quietly.

The assistant stepped closer.

"Sir?"

Kessler didn't look at him.

"It's not an error," he said.

A pause.

"It's a signature."

One that assumes the observer will understand it.

That line is now critical.

He read the sequence again.

Cycle by cycle.

Pressure applied.

Deviation introduced.

Accumulation ensured.

Irreversible.

He understood it now.

Not just what had happened.

How.

And more importantly—

how it would be done again.

He closed the report.

"They didn't break the system," he said.

The assistant remained still.

"They used it."

A brief silence followed.

Then Kessler looked up.

"Forcing compliance through structure," he said.

A pause.

"Elegant."

That word mattered.

Not approval.

Recognition.

Then, more quietly:

"And repeatable."

If allowed to run.

That's your Sting 2 signal.

He stepped away from the desk.

"Prepare a response," he said.

The assistant nodded.

"Scope?"

Kessler considered that.

Then said:

"Measured."

A pause.

"And precise."

He turned back to the display one last time.

"The people involved," he said.

The assistant brought up the associated records.

Names.

Partial identifications.

Fragments.

Kessler studied them.

"They're careful," he said.

"Yes, sir."

"They'll expect retaliation."

A pause.

"Yes, sir."

Kessler gave a faint, almost imperceptible smile.

"Good," he said.

"Let them."

He turned away from the display.

"Begin with the outer layer," he said. "Financial channels. Secondary holdings. Anything they touched."

The assistant nodded.

"And Halvern?"

Kessler didn't hesitate.

"If he surfaces," he said, "we'll address it."

A pause.

"If he doesn't…"

He didn't finish the sentence.

He didn't need to.

The assistant understood.

Kessler moved back to his chair.

Sat.

Calm.

Controlled.

As if nothing had changed.

But everything had.

He looked at the report one last time.

Then closed it.

Quietly.

Deliberately.

"They opened a door," he said.

A brief pause followed.

Then, just as quietly:

"So will I."

And next time—
it won't be theirs to close.

What Happens Next…

The events at Hearthridge did not end when the system shut down.

What Halvern uncovered—and what was set in motion—didn't stay contained. The result was recorded, transmitted, and carried far beyond the site where it began.

And not everyone who receives it will respond the same way.

Some will see it as a failure.

Others will see it as an opportunity.

And a few will understand exactly what it means.

As the consequences begin to spread, the focus shifts outward—beyond controlled systems and defined structures, into places where influence is harder to track and far more dangerous.

New players will emerge.

New environments will test different kinds of control.

And the questions will grow larger:

Who is really in control?

What is being built behind the scenes?

And what happens when the structure itself is no longer enough?

The story continues in

Book 6 — The Perfect Sting

Also by Russell McFall

Ordained Path Books

Clean Science Fiction and Inspirational Writing for Thoughtful Readers

---

A Torlan Tarsen Adventure

- *Character-driven science fiction of leadership, problem-solving, and quiet strength*
- **Torlan Tarsen — Raised Among Giants**
- **Torlan Tarsen — The Havenfall Accord**
- **Torlan Tarsen — The Lost Expedition — Asterra-9**
- **Torlan Tarsen — The Canyon Ascent**
- **Torlan Tarsen — The First Sting**

Contemporary Fiction and Short Stories

Stories of Community, Memory, and Hope

- **Squirrel Creek Estates — Where the Porch Lights Stay On**
- **The World That Chose**

The Space Cadet Richard Series

Where the Legacy Began

- **The Final Countdown**
- **The Dunes of Dinkytown**
- **The Mastermind's Maze**

The Space Cadet Legacy Series

Over 30+ novels of courage, friendship, and discovery — including

- **The First Gate**
- **Welcome Back, Player**
- **Flibber's Journey Home**
- **Stronger Together**
- **Phasegate Rising**
- **The Makers' Handshake**
- **Optimized**

(New missions continuing.)

Literary Humor and Reflections

Serious Nonsense — Sanity Sold Separately

Devotional and Reflection Books

- **Remembering God's Help — Stone by Stone**
- **Attributes of God**
- **This Is My Story, This Is My Song**
- **Lives of Faith**
- **Foundations of Faith**

Russell McFall writes clean fiction and thoughtful reflections designed to uplift the heart, sharpen the mind, and remind every reader that light still wins.

About the Author

Russell McFall is the author of the *Space Cadet Legacy* series, a collection of thoughtful science fiction adventures centered on teamwork, character, and the consequences of choice.

With a background in software development and many years in children's ministry, Russell brings a unique perspective to his writing—blending structured thinking with a heart for clear, meaningful storytelling. His stories began as bedtime adventures for his children and have grown into a series that continues to explore courage, integrity, and leadership.

Russell holds a bachelor's degree from Trinity Bible College and has spent much of his life teaching, mentoring, and encouraging others. He continues to write with the goal of creating stories that are engaging, grounded, and worth returning to.

He lives in the United States and writes daily.

A Note to the Reader

Thank you for taking the time to read this story.

If you enjoyed the journey, a short review—just a few words—can make a real difference. It helps other readers discover the book and decide to give it a try.

And if you'd like to continue the story, more is ahead.

Thank you again for reading.

A Final Thought

Every system works—
until it is tested.

And sometimes, the test doesn't reveal failure.
It reveals something deeper.

Not what the system was designed to do—
but what it becomes under pressure.

In the end, the question is not simply
whether something works.

It is whether it holds—
and what it reveals when it does.

www.ingramcontent.com/pod-product-compliance
Lightning Source LLC
LaVergne TN
LVHW010649110826
845149LV00014B/3002

9781972724170